UNDERCOVER WITCH ACADEMY:

FIRST YEAR

R MEDHURST

Undercover Witch Academy
First Year

Copyright © 2019 by Rachel Medhurst

ISBN: 9781076440310

Published in 2019

This book is dedicated to those who are different...

Other Books in this Series

1

The bedroom door slammed before I could reach it. My eighteenth birthday was not turning into the day I'd hoped it would. If I had to kick down the door to escape, Earth help me, I would.

"Can I ask..." I shouted through the wood. "...why you are keeping me prisoner?"

A grunt from my foster father was followed by a throat clearing from the woman who was supposed to take care of me. Her attempt at being my foster mother had been careless to say the least. I would not be leaving her a five star review once I escaped from the four walls that had trapped me for five years.

"My dear," she started, her sickly sweet tone making me cringe. "You may have come of age, but we need you here. You've become invaluable to us."

"Don't tell her that we've offered her to the institution." Barry's voice was low, but I heard every single disgusting word.

How dare they use my power to gain notoriety, and probably money, for themselves?

Thrusting away from the door, I glanced around my room. I had been waiting for the day that I could escape foster care and start my life. Today was supposed to be that day.

"You don't need to go to any academy, dear, you're safer here!"

Resisting the urge to break down the door with my magic, I grabbed my bag and headed for the window. I had got the offer from the Undercover Witch Academy two days ago. It had been the one I was waiting for, the academy I had to attend.

"I'm sorry," I muttered to my pet stick insects as I thrust open the window and threw my bag to the ground below. "It's time for me to go!"

The ground was two stories down... great, I would have to find a way to get to the grass without breaking a leg. Snapping a bone would hinder my escape, meaning that I would be shipped off to the institute within hours.

It would be easy to mistake me for a schoolgirl, climbing out of her bedroom window, and yet, I was old enough to leave home and attend a university. Why did I always find myself in these bogus situations?

"Alishia, if you don't reply, we're coming in!" my foster father shouted.

Climbing out of the window as the lock clicked, I grasped hold of the ledge and jumped. Whispering a feather spell as I

3

plummeted towards the lawn, I clenched my hands into fists and hoped for the best. My stomach almost touched my throat as I headed for the ground. Just as I was about to hit, my body calmed to a slow descent, the air around me making me weightless.

"That was close," I whispered to myself as my feet touched the soft grass.

Instead of staying upright, I somehow landed in a heap. Typical Alishia, illusionist witch with no magic, and clumsy as hell. Did I say no magic? I meant no magic of my own.

"What are you doing?" the woman who claimed to care for me shouted out of my window.

The urban household only had a small garden, which was handy for me considering the screech of tyres out front. The institute was here... already.

Grabbing my bag, I legged it across the lawn to the gate in the hedge. I flicked it open just as my foster mother screamed my name, alerting the authorities to my whereabouts.

Killing wasn't in my nature, but if the witch - not literally, she was actually human - didn't shut up, I would have to dig into the depths of my darkest nature and end her for good. She deserved it, she only ever fed me chicken nuggets and chips. Surely, a girl deserved better food?

"Alishia!" a man shouted from the end of the small alleyway.

The concrete path ran along the back of the houses, leading to the main street. A train station was across the street and three shops down. I hated urban life, instead preferring the countryside I'd grown up in.

"Wait!"

Ignoring the two agents as they swung into the alley, I raced away from them, down the footpath and towards the traffic. Hopefully, I would be able to get lost in the streets of London. The Undercover Witch

Academy was on the other side of the city and they were expecting me.

My breath rushed in and out as the footsteps behind me quickened. Those chasing me were the top dogs from the institute, a body of paranormal beings who were determined to pluck out the most powerful creatures from the underworld and use them to their advantage. No one knew what they were trying to achieve, but everyone knew that when someone was taken by them, they were never seen again.

"Alishia, stop!"

The cry was urgent, almost kind, and yet, my feet moved faster than they had ever moved before. My magic was low, which meant that I had to get out into the open as soon as I could. They hadn't used their magic, but it wouldn't be long-

A bright blue ball of electric energy crashed into the wooden fence just as I thrust out onto the main street. The sound of cars and people rushed into my ears as I lunged between cars, crossing the road and ignoring the hoots from the drivers.

Managing to get my phone out of my pocket, I glanced over my shoulder to check if they had followed me. They weaved in and out of the people on the pathway, almost shoving them out of the way.

Quickening my pace, I started to run, thanking people when they moved out of the way.

"Isabel?" I said into the phone when my best friend picked up. "They're here. I got the call this morning, so I'm heading to the UWA now. Meet me there."

Not bothering to wait for her reply, I ducked down a side street and yanked open the nearest door. The shop was full of teens just coming out of school. Even though I was only three years older, my height, which was above average, and my bright blonde hair wouldn't blend with the crowd, not to mention the leather jacket and short red dress. Why had I chosen today to wear the brightest colour known to man?

"Can I help you?" a friendly old man asked as I searched for a door, any door.

"I'm desperate for the bathroom," I replied, my gaze locked on the front door of the shop.

The newsagents was small with only two aisles. If the agents came in, I would have to zap some energy from the electric till that the old man stood behind, but I really didn't want to use my power in front of humans.

"There's one just through there... you may use it if you buy something."

The doddery old man pointed a shaky finger to a door that was disguised as a fake shelf. Duh, how had I not seen that? I was about to attend a top academy for training agents, and I hadn't even spotted a hidden door. Great start, Alishia.

"I'll buy the whole shop if you just let me through... please."

Waving me over as a group of teen girls brought chocolate to the till, he dismissed me. Almost lunging behind the counter, I opened the door, checking behind me as it closed. The front door opened and a head of black curly hair started to barge through. It was the woman who had been chasing me.

Her eyes hadn't spotted me before the door clicked shut. My own gaze was on the back door, my legs taking me there before my measly brain could engage. It was a good job I had the same instincts as humans when it came to survival, otherwise I would be a very dead illusionist witch.

The door opened easily as I slipped out silently. If I didn't hurry, they would catch up to me. I had taken a serious risk by coming through the shop. I didn't have a clue whether or not it was enclosed out the back, but I had visited the shop many times, so a part of me felt like it was a sanctuary.

Metal steps led up to the roof. Treading them two at a time, I flew up them, wishing I had a lighter backpack and more magic.

An illusionist witch didn't have a direct line into Mother Earth, we had to steal energy to transform into magic. We were the lowest of the low on the witch hierarchy. Well, except me. Apparently, I had invented a way for us to use magic without stealing it from other witches. Whoopie do.

The crash of the door below forced my head out of my arse as I ran across the balcony that lined the roof. My heart was in my throat as I approached the edge of the building, preparing to jump to the flat roof opposite. Apparently, I wanted to die today.

"Alishia, we only want to talk!" the male agent called from the steps.

Taking a running jump, I managed to soar over the boundary and land on my feet on the grit and stones that lined the roof. Not stopping, I headed straight for the next one, although right at the last minute, an electric cable caught my eye.

Twisting to the left, I dove for the cable at the same time as the man's grunt was followed by the crunch of gravel behind me. He was catching up.

"Stop!" he shouted as my fingers wrapped around the electric cable, and I puffed into thin air.

My whole body shook as it landed in a bush at the side of a road. The leaves scratched me as I thrust around, trying to assimilate the electrical charge that had blasted my body. Most witches would die if they had clung to an electric cable, but not Alishia Jones. Nope, she had found the invention that would almost get her killed. Yes, I was thinking in third person...

Lying still, I listened to the sound of voices on the road outside my hideout. The agents wouldn't be able to follow me here, which was another plus to being me. They couldn't use my connection to Mother Earth - because I didn't have one - to cast location spells. It was no wonder all the academies wanted me. Not because I was super amazingly amazing, but because I was dangerous. What was the best way to beat danger? Control it.

My phone vibrated in my pocket. Tugging it out, I cursed the size of the bloody thing. Why did they have to make them the size of a book? It was a pet peeve that had me leaving my phone in my bag almost all the time.

"I'm here," I said, coughing when my voice almost choked.

"How? You literally phoned me five minutes ago."

Clambering into a sit, I pushed and shoved the bush, trying to get it to do as I pleased. It ignored me, scratching and pushing back. Who knew leaves could be so stubborn?

Whispering, I looked out to check if there was anyone around. "I used an electric cable. I can see you by the gates, I'll be there in two."

Forcing myself out from my hiding place, I pushed my phone into my pocket and casually righted my backpack, tucking my hair behind my ear as I joined my friend.

"You sound like you've run a marathon... and look like you've had a fight with a bush."

Brushing my hair with my fingers, I shrugged as I glanced at the building behind the gates. "I've basically done both over the last few minutes."

The towering medieval academy stood on a risen hill, overlooking London. A park surrounded the sides and back, with the front exposed to the city's old streets. The cobbles were hard under my feet as I glanced at my friend.

"Are you going to tell me what happened?"

Watching the students in their partial uniforms - some wore blazers, some wore skirts, but most matched their uniforms with normal clothes - milling through the gates, I was tempted to hold back and not tell her that the institute had tried to take me. We had known each other since we were born, our mothers had been best friends. Our families had lived next door to one another, so as we grew up, we almost merged into one big extended family. Things had been wonderful, until my parents were killed.

"I've moved out…"

Frowning, Isabel tossed her glossy black hair and tilted her head to the side. Sometimes I wondered if my best friend would still hang out with me if we hadn't known each other growing up. Her deep brown eyes slanted up at the edges, showing her Chinese heritage. Her tall slim figure made me hate her, especially when it was dressed in a pink Harijuku dress paired with

14

the black academy blazer. My red dress clashed with her baby pink, and yet, she wore hers so effortlessly. Me, on the other hand, well... let's just say, I was constantly tugging mine down in an attempt to hide my legs.

"Oh..." a deep voice said behind me as I hoisted my heavy backpack. "I know those legs anywhere."

Turning, I stared at the man who had spoken. I had never seen him before, so how did he know what my legs looked like?

"Dracian!" Isabel almost squealed, shoving my side as she flew past me and flung her arms around the dark haired beauty. I mean, boy... man, whatever.

Wait... Dracian... I knew that name, he was the sole reason I wanted to attend the Undercover Witch Academy. I had never met him, but rage burned my soul as heat licked my skin.

"You shouldn't be staring at my legs, you perv!" Isabel joked, punching him playfully on the arm. "Your girlfriend might not like it."

Laughing, Dracian rested his arm over Isabel's shoulders. Her eyes danced as she turned them to face me. I knew that look, it was a warning bell that I had learnt to listen to.

Taking a deep breath, I clung to the handles of my backpack, waiting for her to speak. My gaze avoided the curly, dark-haired, blued eyed witch. If I looked at him, he might see that I knew who he was or what he had done five years ago.

"This, my dear Dracian," Isabel said, wiggling her eyebrows at me. "Is Alishia Jones."

The witch had been staring at my friend. With the mention of my name, his gaze snapped to mine and... shit, I couldn't look away. Nope, our gaze was locked like one of those mushy teen films where instant love hit. Except, there was no love involved. No, he could probably feel the hatred that rolled from me, towards his Nikes, where it would crawl up and swallow him whole. Hopefully.

"The infamous Miss Illusionist."

Huh?

"Yep. She's started Undercover today."

Reaching for me, she indicated that I should take her hand. Her hyperactive friendly nature grated on my depressive mood. Why couldn't she be sad for a change?

"Pleased to meet you." Throwing him a smile that probably looked more like a wince, I went to move away. "I've got to get to my dorm."

Isabel was about to protest when Dracian let go of her and stood in my path. "My best friend is an illusionist witch. He's spoken about you a lot. I... I'd like to see your skills."

What was I? A magic show? A fucking science experiment?

"Yeah, maybe," I replied, waving at Isabel as I swerved around the witch who watched me closely. "See you later, Iz."

Before I had a chance to get far, Isabel was beside me. She linked an arm through mine as we walked through the gates and approached the steps that led up to the main building. The dorms were in the right wing, according to the email I had received, and the classrooms were in the left. Apparently, the big ballroom in the centre of the academy was for public functions and academy meetings.

"Why does it feel like we're walking into an unholy place?"

Isabel baffled me sometimes. She was a witch, and no witch was religious, and yet, she sometimes came out with the strangest things relating to all different types of religions.

The steps were stone, the bottom a large semi-circle, the rest decreasing in size as they reached the top of the portico. Students filtered through the tall wide wooden doors. They were set in a half oval, the black hinges reminiscent of the medieval age it was built in.

"Anyway..." Isabel let go of me as we ascended the steps. "You need to tell me what-"

Her sentence dropped off as we walked through the doors.

Bloody hell, we had arrived in a palace. My mind stopped obsessing over Dracian as I stared up at the vaulted ceiling that rose into a glass dome. The sunlight dropped through, highlighting the orbs of crystals that floated in the air. Whoever had cast the spell to keep them afloat had made sure that the sun hit them at the perfect angle. As they were highlighted, rays of colour bounced off them, forming a pentagram in mid-air.

"Those steps are divine!" Running towards them, Isabel took out her phone.

The stone steps curved around the circular walls, one on each side of the entrance hall, leading to a platform above. Directly in front of me, more double doors opened into the ballroom. Witches flitted in and out, their expressions full of joy and excitement.

My dead heart just stared as Isabel took selfies with the steps behind her. What was it with my generation? Although, the orbs were pretty, to be fair.

Taking out my phone, I turned it and took a selfie of me under the orbs and coloured pentagram. Okay, so shoot me, I was into the prettiness of the place.

"First day at the academy... and post." Isabel laughed when she returned, her eyes glued to her phone as she obviously shared her picture on one of the social media platforms.

My chest squeezed as a surge of envy climbed over me. I had wanted a normal life, obsessing over magic, books, all things witch, and even having social media. Unfortunately, I hadn't been allowed to join Witchlife.org. The social media platform was one of the top places to share spells, photos and all things witchery.

According to the site, a witch could only join after a check had been run to make sure that you weren't human. The human world wasn't supposed to know about paranormals, but that secret hadn't stayed completely hidden. Some humans craved the nuance of the underworld. The dark held a lot of appeal for them, apparently. I couldn't see why.

"Now that you're here," Isabel said. "You can use your academy credentials to join Witch Life."

I had been refused because of my status as an *Illusionist Witch*. There was a ton of prejudice against those of us who had no magic of our own. We were scary to other witches. We could syphon magic and create illusions with it. If I wanted to fool someone into thinking I looked a certain way, I could steal some magic and change my appearance. It was a handy skill to have, but it left others not trusting me. I could kind of see their point, especially as I was the type of person to use it. Who wouldn't want to be someone else for the day? It was fun.

"Registration is through there," Dracian said as he passed, pointing towards the ballroom. "You better get a move on before they change their mind."

Flicking Isabel's hair, Dracian winked at me as he joined his friends and made his way inside. Why did it feel like I was a schoolgirl going to Hogwarts? I was eighteen, surely I should be feeling more grown up than a high-schooler?

"I'm not sure this was such a good idea." Marching towards the hall, I didn't wait for

Isabel to catch up to me. "But, I have something to do here."

"You do?" my best friend said, pulling me to a stop.

Staring at Dracian's back, I vowed to keep my promise to my mother. She had lain dying in my arms five years ago, almost to the day. Her death had been caused by a spell cast by someone else. My father had succumbed to the spell, too, joining her on the other side at the same time.

"Okay, time to stop dodging my question. What happened today?"

Looking around, I smiled at a girl who made eye contact at the wrong time. It was so awkward when that happened, and yet, we British just smiled shyly and looked away. There was no way we would dare speak to a person, it just wasn't the British way. It certainly wasn't my way either, but freedom was upon me, I was going to make the most of it.

Tugging Isabel into the corner, I watched the students file in as I told her about my foster parents shopping me in to the institute. "I ran as fast as I could when they turned up. Luckily, I found the perfect magical source to blast me out of there. Otherwise, the bastards would've got me. I hate to think what they do there. Impregnation, oh, or what's the one where they shove things up your-?"

"Okay, stop!" Isabel almost gagged, her cringe written all over her screwed up face. "Why does your brain go off on weird tangents like that?"

"You're telling me you haven't thought about what the institute does to witches before they disappear?"

Shaking her pretty head, Isabel raised her perfectly plucked eyebrows. Oh to have the luxury of worrying about hairs that sat above the eyes. What were they for anyway? Why did we have hair on our brow bone?

A scream from the girl who had smiled at me caught our attention. She stared at the balcony above, her hand slowly raising to point. Her free hand covered her mouth as her eyes widened.

Moving away from the side of the room, we looked to see what she was so afraid of. My own hand went to my chest when I saw that a girl was standing on the stone banister, reaching for the orbs that lit up the dome.

"Come down!"

A girl next to her was desperately trying to get her friend to safety. The stupid friend, yes, anyone who stood on the top of a stone banister and reached for a shiny object must be pretty stupid. Or maybe...

Looking at the girl's eyes, I swore under my breath. Her eyes were wide, unblinking, vacant. Someone had put a spell on her. Someone must have suggested that she take an orb. Who would do such a thing and why?

"Don't worry," Isabel shouted to the girl. "I can catch her if she falls."

The thundering of footsteps alerted us to the presence of a short woman with very high heels. Her short pixie cut showed a long neck and small chin. Her big green eyes blinked as she came out of the ballroom, spun on her heels and stared up at the girl, who was still reaching for the orb, somehow managing to balance precariously.

"Young girl, you might think that you can fly like a fairy, but you're a witch. Get down now, or I'll throw you out of the academy." Her clipped voice was sweet, and yet, it held a bite of something sharp underneath.

I instantly liked her.

Of course, the student ignored her as she stuck her tongue out and clasped it between her lips. She inclined even further forward, making the students who had gathered gasp loudly.

Going over to the woman who was inspecting her fingernails, I tapped her gently on the shoulder. "Excuse me, miss."

"Miss?" She laughed, her big beaming smile transforming her face. "I love that you think I'm young enough to be a Miss. I'm Professor Hinley, but you can call me Mrs Hinley. I would offer to shake your hand, but I'm due a manicure and that student is about to jump."

"She's spelled," I replied, not bothering to acknowledge any of the other stuff she'd said.

The teacher's gaze snapped back to the girl above us. Pursing her lips, she whispered a spell under her breath and clicked her fingers. Nothing happened. Her brows pulled low in a frown.

"That didn't work." My muttered words afforded me a narrowed gaze.

"Something's not right. Come with me!"

Marching towards the stairs, she ran up them two at a time. Her frame was slightly larger, but she didn't puff as she hurried. Her glamourous mumsie look, if there could be such a thing, was a farce, meant to lull students into a false sense of safety.

Following her, I trotted up the steps just behind. Her high heels clattered on the stone as she reached the top and headed straight for the girl.

"Get down!" she commanded in a high pitched voice.

Again, she was ignored as the girl stretched higher and higher.

Whispers echoed around the whole hallway as more and more students came to see what was going on.

"Mrs Hinley?" I said, quietly trying to gain her attention.

"Someone go and get the headmaster, he'll know what to do," she said, waving her hands in no particular direction. "If she touches them, it will give her an electric shock and kill her."

Without waiting to speak to her, I moved closer to the girl. She was straining now, her teeth clenching so hard on her tongue, blood dripped down her chin.

"You can't touch someone in an inducement spell," Mrs Hinley said as I inched even closer.

Every witch in the academy would know that rule. If we jolted someone out of a spell where they had lost the ability to control themselves, they could jump out of their body altogether. Or their soul could. I didn't fully understand it, 'cos you know, I hadn't done so well in magic arts at my high school, but I got the gist.

Grabbing onto the banister, I pulled myself up, almost toppling straight over the edge before I managed to get my balance.

Mrs Hinley had a hissy fit behind me, flapping like a duck. "What are you doing, child? You're not helping at all!"

Tuning out the rush of gasps and the incessant nagging of the professor, I closed my eyes and caught my balance. Okay, so I was risking everything, but you know... a girl had to act. If I didn't, the student next to me would probably fall to her death. Her legs were starting to shake, and yet, she still persevered.

Opening my eyes, I pushed myself up and lunged forward. Screams echoed around me as I flew through the air, grasped the orange orb nearest to us and started to plummet. The electric magic thudded through me, sending my power metre up. Absorbing it, I whispered a levitation spell.

"Shitting hell," I heard Isabel say to a boy standing next to her. "That's my friend."

Another shout alerted me to what I had feared. The sound of the girl falling hit my ears just as she passed me. The wind from her fall dragged me down, but I shouted the same spell as I caught her arm with my hand.

The girl started to float, her body slowing down and coming into line with mine as we landed. I wasn't able to lift my legs properly in time, so we both thudded on the ground gently.

A scream came from the girl as she snapped out of her trace. Thrashing on the ground, she pushed me away, her hysteria getting out of control. Her whole body started to seize, her muscles shaking her so violently, her eyes rolled into the back of her head.

"Move out of the way!" Mrs Hinley called as she jostled through the students who surrounded us. "I must get to them."

Isabel was beside me, helping me to my feet. Stepping back, I stared at the girl before looking down at the orb. What was it about the shiny ball that had made someone cast a spell for the girl to grab it? Why was she currently fitting on the stone floor?

I could feel the intensity of magic from the orb as it pulsed through me, but it wasn't any stronger than a normal magic spell. Who would harm another student to get it?

"You'd better give me that," a stern masculine voice boomed.

Turning, I blinked as I pushed the magic through my fingertips and into the orb.

Mrs Hinley calmed the student with a sedation spell, sending her back into a trance-like state.

I wasn't sure if it was wise to make her comatose again, but who was I to judge? Oh yeah, the girl who had just saved her life.

"She… she's almost lost her magic," Mrs Hinley stuttered loudly.

Gasps resounded around the hallway as students backed up, their eyes glancing at the orb. No, it hadn't been me, I was out of magic. Almost. I reminded myself that they didn't know that I was an illusionist witch, so I was safe from their judgement. For now.

"Who are you?" A tall, silver-grey-haired man approached me, wiggling his fingers.

Before I could reply, students parted, almost dashing out of the hallway in all directions. The orb left my hands, flying across the way and into his hands.

"My name is Alishia Jones," I replied, standing firm when he came to tower over me.

His long legs were encased in black denim jeans, his torso covered by a rock T-shirt, the edges frayed and metal rings clanging as he moved. I couldn't help but imagine the guitar probably hidden in his music room at the academy. The old toff probably couldn't play it at all but liked to think he could.

"My dad liked ACDC. I'm more of a Nirvana fan myself."

Blinking, he sloped his head to look at me. "I knew your father from our own academy days. He was a good man." Turning to Mrs Hinley, he raised his eyebrows. "Take her to the infirmary, I'll speak to Miss Jones."

As he spoke, Dracian Dread came out of the ballroom, winking at me as he headed towards the dorm wing.

I kept my face straight as a surge of heat raced through my veins. How dare the boy who had hurt my family be so callous?

"Thank you, sir," I replied, bringing my attention back to the professor as he spun the orb in his hand. An unexpected surge of sadness made me swallow hard.

"What just happened? Did you - you know?" Waving his hand at the student before Mrs Hinley disappeared with her, he nodded his head.

"No! I used the magic from the orb," I whispered. "I promise I was just trying to help."

Narrowing his gaze on me, he pointed towards the ballroom. "My name is Professor Seaton. We'll speak more about this later. You better get registered before the books close. Welcome to the Undercover Witch Academy, Alishia Jones, it's a pleasure to meet you."

2

"Why am I in a different room?" I asked Isabel as she came out of her lodgings.

The dorms were typical for a university or academy. Room after room with two people of the same gender. I had been instructed to join my new roommate, but I had managed to keep Isabel from leaving me for two hours. She was getting weary, ready to move in and explore her new home.

"Don't worry," she said, waving as she closed her door. "I'm right here."

Standing in the middle of the white painted hallway, I stared back where I had come from. Dark wood lined the walls midway, but the rest of the place had nowhere near as much character as the main building.

Disappointment almost made me leave. When I had seen the pictures of the academy online, I had been excited to explore its corridors. How could a medieval building have so little character in the dorm rooms? How could I pretend to be in a gothic horror movie if there was no ambience?

Saying that, was that a shadow at the end of the hall? The flick of the lights made my spine straighten. When they were on again, the shadow had gone. Shuddering, I shook myself of ridiculous notions.

"Excuse me?" a friendly voice called from the door to my room.

Bracing myself, I turned to see a girl around the same height as me with long curly waves down her back. Now, *she* had

37

the type of hair to get away with being in a gothic horror film.

"Do you ever wonder why we signed up to do this?" she asked, opening the door wider so I could enter.

Walking into the room, I stared at the decoration on her side. She had a bookcase full of fiction and witch self-help books. Man, she even had the one I had asked for from my foster family. "Dudette, I've been dying to read *Seven Ways to Kill a Witch*. I figure if anyone wants to kill me, they'll need to be versed in the practice of killing a witch, so why not learn how to look for the signs."

"Er..." The girl blinked rapidly as she un-enthusiastically waved towards the case. "You can borrow it, I guess. Although, why would someone want to kill you?"

"Because they killed my parents."

My reply left her baffled, just like a goldfish as it sat in its bowl, day in, day out, its little mouth opening and closing. Maybe I shouldn't have shared such vital information. Silly, Alishia!

"My name's Alishia Jones." After taking out the book, I went over to her and held out my hand.

It was better to be polite to the witch I would be sleeping next to. If she was going to kill me in my sleep, being nice to her might make it harder. Killing a kind girl would make her feel guilty. Not that I had a complex about getting killed. Much.

Clearing her throat as she took my hand gingerly, the girl summoned up a fake smile. "I'm Helissa Wayward."

Almost choking, I turned my gaze to stare at her. I had been admiring her *Witch Way is the Best Way* poster just behind her head, but her name made me want to bow down. Now it was my turn to be the fish in a bowl. "As in... The Weird Wayward witches? The inspiration for Shakespeare's witches?"

Nodding slowly, Helissa tucked her hair behind her ear as she looked at the ground. "The very same. A bloody annoying name to live up to, I'm afraid. Don't expect good things. I'm literally here because of my bloodline, not because I'm any good at magic."

"I know how you feel," I muttered, going over to my bed and dumping my backpack.

"Are you the illusionist witch who invented a way for your kind not to steal magic from other witches?"

Glancing over my shoulder, I narrowed my eyes on Helissa. She was as blunt as I was, that was a bonus. I hadn't met many people who were upfront. Maybe the academy would be better than I had thought. Two new people I liked... both women, naturally. And two men I didn't like... at all.

"I'm the very same witch, yes. Don't worry, I won't be nicking your magic in the night."

Going to the window, I watched the students as they formed groups on the grass, introducing themselves and settling into the new school year. This is what it must have felt like to go to a boarding school. My parents had been on the verge of sending me to one when they were killed. I had escaped that hideousness when I went into foster care. It was the one and only saving grace of their death. Cold? Yes, it was. I couldn't help it, it was the only thing I could hold on to that didn't make me fall apart.

"The whole place knows what you did to save that girl in the entrance hall."

No matter what happened in the academy, it would always feel like a school, so I had to come to terms with that. Why not embrace the bitchiness, the comparison, and the utter disregard of others emotions? How else would I survive as a student of magic?

Moving to my bed, I stared at the unmade mattress. The institute and my foster parents had chased me out before I could make any arrangements. I didn't even have sheets on my cover, let alone a change of clothing. Most witches would be able to magic up new outfits and decorate half-dorm rooms, but me? The magic I cast with borrowed energy wasn't as powerful as that, so I had limited options.

"I can... I mean... I..." Helissa waved towards my side of the room, staring at my glaringly small backpack.

Smiling, I shook my head. "Thanks for the offer, but I've got to head out."

Grabbing up my bag, I rushed from the room before my roommate could reply. It was mortifying that I had nothing to my infamous name. A girl had to do what a girl had to do, which was why I made my way out of the building, searching for an establishment that served alcohol.

Students watched me as I left the grounds, striding through the gates as if I didn't just perform the perfect illusionist witch spell. If only they knew who I really was. Although, saying that, it was probably best they didn't. I was just as bland as my magic most days. Some days, my imagination took me on trips that others would enjoy if they were with me.

Laughter burst from my lips at my own thoughts. A passing boy smiled at me, his cheeks burning bright red when I grinned back. I didn't have any interest in engaging much with the opposite sex... well, except for the cute boy that had walked past, winking at me... he was right up my street.

"Excuse me." He stopped me, pointing towards the academy as he spoke. "Is that the Undercover Witch Academy?"

Smiling, I glanced at the ground before lifting my head. No, why should I be shy around him? I was Alishia Jones, kickass woman, ready for...ah, who was I kidding... "Ermm... yeah, that's the academy."

Thanking me with one of those annoyingly coy grins that sent girl's weak at the knees, he waved as he moved away.

My sigh was loud before I snapped out of it and headed towards the pub on the corner of the park. I was eighteen years old, far too old to fawn over male witches. Why was I checking over my shoulder to see if his retreating butt was still in sight?

"Watch it!" A grouchy voice fell into my ears as I bumped into someone.

My fingers brushed the man's wrist as I pushed away from him. Tingling tickled the skin of my fingertips as his magic filtered into me.

"What are you doing?" he snapped as he threw his cigarette on the ground.

The bar was right behind him, the door propped open to allow the air to move through. I considered ignoring him and diving inside without explanation, but I hadn't been brought up to be rude. My parents had always made sure I apologised, especially when I accidentally stole someone's magic. It had been extremely careless. See, that's why boys were trouble!

"I'm so sorry." Going to take his hand in apology, I bit my lip when he stepped away. "I was in a rush."

Nodding, he dismissed me with a shake of the head. When I went to walk into the Rose and Crown, he called me back. "Where are you going?"

"Huh?" My dumbfounded look must have made him feel sympathy for me because his expression softened.

"This is my pub. You don't look old enough to drink."

Oh crap, I had literally just insulted the barman, I mean manager, before I had even got into the pub. The chances of him giving me a job was slim to none. Especially if he believed I looked too young, too.

"I'm eighteen. I'm actually looking for a job."

Coughing, he shook his head as he indicated that I follow him inside. Once through the door, the atmosphere pressed down on me.

The clientele were droll, old men who nursed a beer in the middle of the afternoon. A couple of students sat in the corner, their pints and shots piled on the table. If I worked here, it might make me even more depressed than I had been in foster care.

"Come out back," the manager said, picking up the wooden bar divider and waiting for me to go through. "I'm Frankie, by the way."

Hesitating, I swallowed as I checked to see if anyone watched us. If he attacked me, I would at least have witnesses here, but-

"Forget the thoughts you have of all the bad things I might do to you. You're not my type."

Smiling to myself, I ducked through the gap and followed him through a door at the back of the bar. Music filtered into me as I emerged into another bar. Bright orange lights illuminated the chairs and tables, giving it the look of flames running down the walls.

"Wait... what's this room for?"

As I spoke, a group of students, clutching bags with the academy crest emblazoned on it, walked in. They laughed as a holographic image of the man standing next to me appeared in front of them, doing a magic trick with balls and electric fire.

"This is where the magic happens... Literally."

Shaking my head, I watched as the students went over to a table and ordered their drinks. The illusion of the manager waved his hands, nodding when the drinks flew down from the ceiling above.

Inclining his head when they cheered him, the illusion disappeared.

"Why did you bring me in here? You obviously don't need me if you can duplicate yourself to serve."

Crossing my arms over my waist, I watched the students as they laughed and joked together. They must have been in the year above me. Their demeanour was not of a new, nervous student coming to the academy for the first time.

"You're an illusionist witch, like me."

His simple reply made me turn to him. He watched me, his gaze studying my reaction. Ever since my father had helped me invent a way for me to use magic without stealing it, I had learnt how to hide my feelings. I knew that my face was blank, not telling him anything. There was a special skill in performing illusion magic.

"And?"

Shrugging, the man moved to the bar that lined the back wall and poured himself a juice. Offering me one, he smiled when I grudgingly accepted. What? I was thirsty, I needed to hydrate. Even if it meant staying in a place that could potentially become dangerous. It was very rare to meet another illusionist witch. Most were elemental. I had to be careful.

"I figured that this is your first day of school-"

"Uni," I interjected, terribly offended that he thought I looked young enough to be in school.

Waving away my words, he handed me the juice and turned to face the bar again. There was a pool table in the corner with a myriad of coloured balls. I had never seen the game, but it looked like it had been modified for witches.

"If you're in here on the first day of... uni..." He winked at me, smiling when I glared intensely at him, letting him know with the daggers shooting out of my eyes that he wasn't funny. At all. "I know you need the money. So... I'm prepared to give you a trial run. It's quiet this afternoon, I'll give you a lesson in bartending."

Looking at the students who laughed between themselves, I ignored the pang that had me wanting to join them. To act normal and pretend to be an ordinary person without the confines of my parents' murder or my international status of infamous *Illusionist Witch*.

"That's great," I answered, probably looking a little less than enthusiastic. "Where's the beer?"

3

The scream jolted me awake. Thrusting up from my unmade bed, I switched on the bedside lamp that had appeared when I had been out. My heart jumped into my chest as I took in the scene in front of me.

Helissa was pointing at the tank at the end of her bed. Someone was retreating from the room, her familiar in their hand.

"Has he just stolen your snake?" I asked, jumping out of bed.

The girl nodded, tears trembling at the corners of her eyes as she clutched her cover.

Tripping over my boots, which I'd carelessly left in the middle of the room, I rushed from the room, straight through the open door.

The hooded figure was wearing baggy blue denim jeans, his back retreating down the corridor, towards the entrance-hallway.

"Stop!" I shouted, charging after him.

I hadn't bothered to absorb any energy or electricity the night before, not believing I'd need it in the middle of the night. That was the problem with illusionist witches, we couldn't just cast a spell to help us when we needed it, we had to obtain magic first.

My bare feet slapped the wooden lino floor as I pumped my arms, trying to get some speed behind me. Air blasted in and out of my lungs. Why was I so bad at running? Or any sport for that matter?

"What's going on?" someone shouted from behind me.

Ignoring them, I thundered after the kidnapper - wait, no, they were a familiar-napper - that didn't sound quite right, but whatevs. The culprit swung around the end of the hall, heading for the stairs. I pushed all my energy into my legs, begging them to keep working as they protested.

"Alishia?" A deep voice spoke before Dracian Dread stepped out of a room, his whole form bashing straight into me.

My momentum kept me going, sending me flying to the ground, my palms grazing the floor. Footsteps faded away as the person who had taken Helissa's familiar disappeared down the stairs. I landed in a heap at the end of the corridor, just catching sight of the snake before they vanished.

"Are you okay?"

Looking up from under my hair, I scowled at Dracian.

He stood by his door, not bothering to come and see if I was hurt. Had the bastard stopped me on purpose? By the smug expression on his pretty face, I suspected that he had. His dark eyes flicked between my face and my legs. Why was he staring at-? Oh.

Giggles rent the air as several witches came out of their rooms. Men on one side, women the other. My nightdress, which was basically a T-shirt, had risen up to my boobs. It was a good job I had worn knickers to bed, otherwise they would all be getting a view that I would never live down. It was bad enough as it was.

"Alishia!" Helissa hurried down the corridor, heading straight for me. "Did you catch them?"

Grumbling as I got up from my heap, I shook my head. Did it look like I had caught them? Was the snake in my arms and the culprit dead on the floor? No? That meant he had gotten away. "No, I didn't, I'm sorry."

"What happened?" one of the male witches asked as he eyed up my legs.

"None of your business," I snapped back, pointedly staring at the bulge between his legs. Two could play that game, although when he strutted towards us, I realised my mistake. Men were a whole different breed.

Raising his eyebrows, he turned to a sobbing Helissa. "Are you okay?"

She sniffled as she shook her head, falling into his arms when he opened them. Seriously? What...? I mean... Why...? Ugh, I would never understand the weakness of women when it came to men. Or the arrogance of men when it came to women. It was a concept I had yet to fathom. Although, as the boy patted Helissa's arm, I couldn't help but admire the movement of the muscles on his back. It was a- No, just, no.

"Someone stole my familiar. They snuck in and took Toby."

"Toby?" the boy and I said in unison, smiling at each other when our gaze met.

My gaze moved to Dracian as he pushed away from the wall he'd been leaning on. "I'll go and see if I can find them," he offered, touching Helissa's arm as he passed, all of a sudden in a rush to be away from us.

"Thank you!" Helissa called as he went to trot down the stairs.

None of them could see him, it still being slightly dark in the corridor, but I watched as he looked over his shoulder at me. Was that a smirk on his face? Had he come out of his room on purpose? I knew that he was evil, his actions when it came to my parents' death spoke louder than anything, but I had no proof. I had come to the Undercover Witch Academy, not only to become a kickass witch agent, but to out Dracian Dread and avenge my parents' murder.

"Alishia?" Helissa nudged me in the arm. "Will you come with me to report this to the head professor?"

"Now?" I said, looking down at my bare legs.

Nodding, Helissa sobbed, her face crumpling in on itself like a discarded screwed up piece of paper. I had never had a familiar because, you know, I wasn't exactly a proper witch according to most other witches, so I had no idea about the pain she would be feeling. Except... my chest squeezed hard as an image of my mother's face slunk into my mind.

Shoving it away before tears could erupt, I grabbed Helissa's arm and dragged her back to our bedroom, where I quickly donned a pair of leggings. My dressing gown was next. We were going to visit the main man of the academy; I didn't want to look anything but my best... in my nightclothes.

"Oh my goddess," Isabel cried as she came running into the room. "I've just heard what happened. Did you see who it was?"

Looking between the pair of us, she flapped, not sure who to go to.

Well, it wasn't my familiar that was stolen, so I didn't need the sympathy. Although, I had been given a fright by Helissa's screaming, so...

"We need to go to the professor," I interrupted when it looked like Isabel was just going to stand and stare at the empty tank.

Taking Helissa's arm, Isabel managed to soothe her as we made our way out of the room.

Other witches were still hanging around, discussing what had happened. It was typical that I had been the centre of two escapades only a day into the first year. I had wanted to keep my head down, out of everyone's way, until I was ready to out

Dracian Dread and get my revenge. However, my wishes had not been commanded.

My feet dragged behind the pair as they chattered together, apparently swapping stories about their familiars. It wasn't a conversation I could join with, which made me a little sad. Seeing my best friend laughing with another girl made me watch the stone tiles as we descended the steps to the main entrance hall.

Glancing up, I frowned as I caught sight of something black before it disappeared. The stairs in the right dorm wound up, leading to the dorms of the higher years. There were four floors altogether, although the top floor was reserved for VIP students.

"Alishia's illusions are amazing," Isabel was saying. "She can create beautiful clothes with the click of her finger. Of course, when the magic wears off, the clothes disappear, but it's fun all the same!"

Helissa looked over her shoulder at me as she attempted to tuck a piece of her wildly curly hair behind her ear. "That sounds fun."

Her grief made her words seem insincere, but as she smiled kindly, I smiled back, pushing away the normal reactions that would usually come from my mouth.

Isabel hadn't been around me as much in the last few years. Her parents had offered to adopt me when my parents died, but the institute put a stop to it. My parents had encouraged me with my experiments, ignoring the calls to tame me from those higher up.

"When we get Toby back, we'll er... well, you know, I'll show you."

The entrance hall was dark as we entered. The bright light from the orbs reflected down, casting coloured shadows, but the darkness was still oppressive as we crossed to the other side of the building, slipping into the corridor of the lesson wing. The teachers' quarters were away from the classes, down a corridor immediately on our right.

The scratching of something behind us made me turn, searching the entrance hallway before I followed the others. No one was there, but the light flickered more than it had when we'd walked under it. Was there someone there? What insane person would walk around a medieval building in the middle of the night? Oh yeah... me.

"I think this is his room," Helissa whispered.

A plaque with the professor's name was fixed to the wall beside the wooden door.

The whole hallway was made up of wooden walls and stone flooring, evidently the oldest part of the building. A tingle went up my spine as I looked at an old-fashioned painting that hung on the wall at the end of the hallway.

"Who's there?" a masculine voice shouted from inside.

We fumbled over ourselves, three witches unable to think of what to say. Before we got ourselves together, the door opened and the metal-head man from earlier grunted in our direction. His greying hair fell to his shoulders, the long strands wispy. His ACDC T-shirt was crumpled where he'd obviously been napping in it. He didn't look like the napping type, despite the aging wrinkles on his face.

"What do you want? Why are you-?"

"My familiar was just kidnapped!" Helissa blurted, her sobbing starting all over again.

And there I was, lost in the history of the place as I imagined women dressed in great big puffy dresses, wandering the halls. Maybe there was a ghost who haunted the halls at night, warning us to stay away from-

"You!" the professor barked, pointing at me. "Why are you involved in yet another misdemeanour? It's been barely a few hours

and you're making a name for yourself already."

Was the professor really picking on me when a crime of the utmost disrespect had taken place? I mean, really... Yes, I might have been present at the two bizarre occurrences of the day, but still... this one had nothing to do with me.

"Alishia," Isabel whispered, pulling me to the side as the professor took the details from Helissa. "Did you cast an illusion to wind up Helissa?"

Frowning, I glared at my friend. "How could you...? Seriously?"

Hearing the professor agree to investigate the snake-napping... yeah, it worked... I stormed away from my friend, ignoring her when she called out to me. How dare she think such a thing? Why would I want to bring pain to someone I didn't even know? Snakes didn't bother me, Helissa had seemed nice so far. What possible cause would I have to pretend to take the familiar?

Seething, I took calm, slow breaths, just as the therapist had taught me after my parents were killed. She had advised me to take nothing personally, and to never allow another human being to have power over my actions and reactions.

Unfortunately, right this moment, I wanted to burn down the school.

Maybe, just maybe, I would. A little fire wouldn't harm anyone...

4

"I'm sorry I accused you last night," Isabel said quietly as we sat at the table. "Please, please, please, tell me you've forgiven me."

Holding out her arms, she tried to pull me into a hug.

Resisting her tugging hands, I laughed gently when she planted a kiss on my cheek, just to annoy me.

"Okay, okay." Glancing around the room, I tried not to roll my eyes at the typical witch classroom.

The walls were still bare, the stone bricks showing the craftsmanship of hundreds of years ago. Wooden tables, laid in lines facing the blackboard at the front. Paintings of famous witches who had graduated from the Academy hung on the walls, bringing gloomy images of men and women who now served as agents in the investigative field.

"Who's our teacher?" I asked, looking at my timetable.

Mrs Hinley. Oh, that was good. Maybe I would have an ally in the teacher, especially after what had happened yesterday.

"I know we're not in high school," Isabel said, nudging me in the side. "But... Dracian's friend is right up my street."

"Up your street? I thought I was the only one who used that antiqued saying. Shouldn't you be describing him as hot?"

Watching as Dracian and another boy settled at a desk a few rows ahead, I tried to study the friend that had caught Isabel's eye.

I failed... miserably. No matter how much I tried to determine how hot he was, my gaze kept slipping to the back of Dracian's head.

A surge of heat flew through me when he glanced over and waved at Isabel. How dare he act like he hadn't done anything?

"How's it going, Alishia Magic Fingers?" he said loudly.

Wait... was he speaking to me? And what the hell had he just called me? If I hadn't seen the CCTV that placed him at my home when my parents were killed, I would've been easily swayed by the dark brown eyes and short wavy hair. No, he was a murderer, a heartless one at that.

Isabel poked me in the ribs, stretching her eyes as if to tell me to answer.

Clearing my throat, I shrugged, ducking my gaze.

"All good?" I called to Helissa when she stumbled into class, dropping her bag on the ground.

The night before, she had arrived back at the room not long after me, treading quietly. I had instantly dived under my covers, snuggling into myself, trying not to cry. My own best friend accused me of casting an illusion that would harm someone. That had always been my rule, I had even signed a promise written by my parents. I shall never use my illusionist magic to hurt or kill another being unless in danger myself.

Shuffling her seat along, Isabel called for Helissa to join us. A part of me scowled on the inside, wishing that I could sit on my own, but the other part caught the genuine smile that my roommate threw my way.

She was just as lost as I was in the new world of witchery. Deciding to train in the arts of investigative magic made her have more in common with me than most witches.

"Morning," she muttered, rubbing her eyes as she settled. "The professor just text to say

he would start the investigation tonight. I...
I..."

Her throat moved as she swallowed, obviously choking back the grief that threatened. I had listened to her cry herself to sleep the night before, unable to offer her the comfort she obviously needed. I wouldn't do that today. I was a good girl, a nice girl... it was time I started acting it. Until someone went over the line, then it all went out the window.

"Tonight?" I said, shaking my head. "That's so wrong. Why is he delaying it? Surely, in an academy full of ex-agents, they must know how to easily find the culprit and bring back Toby the snake?"

Our attention was caught by every student who entered greeting Dracian Dread. Their loud ruckus distracted me as they poured over him, almost adoring his annoying witch-self.

"How does everyone know him?" I asked Isabel.

Looking up from checking her Instagram, Isabel hummed a response, not quite hearing what I had said. When it sunk in, she shook herself and laughed.

"Oh, he set up a ton of get-togethers through the summer so the school year could get to know one another. Of course, you didn't know that you were coming then, so…"

Helissa moved her chair and blocked my view of the boy who had apparently charmed everyone before he had even arrived. I would have a tough job getting close to him. Not in that way, that was disgusting and disturbing considering what he had done. But, I had to get the proof needed to let everyone know who he really was.

"I need your help," Helissa whispered, taking out a piece of dried shed snakeskin.

Isabel went to squeak, but I gripped her wrist and squeezed. "Don't..."

Looking between us, she screwed up her face. "It's gross."

"If you think this is gross..." Helissa paused as she took out a small pouch of salt and a map. "... you wait until we have to peruse a dead body for clues."

Clenching her teeth and stretching her lips, Isabel moaned her disapproval. I stared at her, quite baffled by her response. For months, she had been excited about coming to the academy.

"What did you expect would happen at the Undercover Witch Academy? That we would lounge around and sit under things? Did you think that undercover meant staying in bed, under the duvet? Or that the-?"

"Stop!" Isabel slapped me on the arm, giggling as she bit her lip. "Of course not, I just... I dunno, hoped I could skip that class."

"And you want to be an agent... why?" Helissa asked, laying out the map and spreading salt around it.

Huddling closer together, we tried to hide what we were doing.

Shuddering, Isabel waved away her question and pointed at the flaky transparent snakeskin. "Let's just find the bastard who took Toby. No one has a right to steal someone's familiar, it's against witch law."

"Okay," Helissa whispered, taking Isabel's hand.

When Isabel went to take mine, I raised my eyebrows and pulled my hand away. "Really?"

Tilting her head to the side, Isabel licked her pretty bow lips before she smiled. "Come on!"

Frowning, I glanced around the classroom. When we had been younger, Isabel had been my main source of magic. I had managed to trick my parents into believing that I was a normal witch by taking some of my best friend's magic before I went home from school.

"It's been a while," she said quietly, grabbing my hand before I could move it fast enough.

When Isabel had been sick, my parents had taken me on a weekend break without her family, which meant my source of magic was no longer around. Our holiday had quickly descended into shouting and arguing when they realised that their seven year old had stolen magic daily from her friend... just to please them.

My heart was heavy as I remembered the moment that both our parents had forbid us from ever touching again. If we were ever caught sharing magic, we would be separated. Isabel's mother was traditionally Chinese, her hopes in her daughter going far in life far outweighing her love for me. Or rather, her reason was better than her emotional reaction. She knew that illusionist witches were frowned upon. Their inability to connect to Mother Earth and the ley lines meant that most covens believed that there was something inherently wrong with the witch.

Gritting my teeth, I fought back the grief that washed over me. From that day forward, my parents worked with me to try and find a way that I could safely syphon magic without taking it from other witches.

"Mrs Hinley will be here in a minute," Helissa hissed as the other students chatted amongst themselves.

Dracian kept facing forward, not bothering with the likes of us, instead laughing with a pretty witch who had French plaits down each side of her head. Apparently, she hadn't got the memo about the academy being for grownups.

"Okay." My tentative agreement made Isabel's eyes well up.

Shaking her hand, I swallowed as I pulled magic from her. The parts of her skin that my fingertips touched warmed, the blast so familiar and yet, a distant memory. I had vowed never to use another person's magic when my parents had died. Why was I now breaking that vow? Helissa wasn't exactly my best, *get locked up in jail for*, friend.

Isabel, on the other hand... she was... Even if we hadn't seen much of each other over the last five years. We had a bond that was as strong as family.

"It tickles." She laughed, her face softening when our gazes met.

She was remembering the happy time, too. A time that we could never get back.

Bending her head, Helissa started to silently chant the location spell. Her lips moved quickly as she touched the dry snakeskin with her free hand. I studied her

75

tanned skin and the thick dark lashes that sat against her cheeks where she had her eyes closed. I could see why the boy had comforted her last night. Her innocence shouted loud and clear, but her beauty was understated. A regular girl, just like us.

"What are you doing?" A masculine voice made us jump.

Dracian appeared behind me, staring at the map. A chill went down my spine as his dark eyes traced the salt, and then the snakeskin, smirking when it clicked. Great, the popular boy knew what we were doing. If he said anything, I would-

"Want some help?"

Taking my hand, he frowned when I ripped away from him, almost releasing Isabel. The salt slowly started to move, a fine line of it extending onto the map. The spell was working. Oh great, I had to sit, extremely uncomfortably, might I add, and let a boy who had called me Magic Fingers, watch me do my thing.

"Oh yeah," Dracian, the Dread, whispered. "I forgot…"

Leaving me alone, he put his hand on Isabel's shoulder and ducked his head, closing his eyes as he offered us his magic.

Using Isabel's magic to intensify the spell, I allowed it to run through me and back into her.

No one had ever known why a select few witches were born without magic. It had been a phenomenon that no coven had ever managed to explain. A witch from the Salem line in America had been the first man to realise that he could syphon magic from other witches when he took a witch lover. It had always been frowned upon for illusionist witches to marry. They were regarded as human, even if they'd come from witch parents. The mixing of witches, warlocks and humans was prohibited by the human government and had been forever, just so they could control us all as individual species.

"It's stopped." Isabel dropped my hand and pointed at the spot where the salt formed into a pile over a location.

"Okay, class!" Mrs Hinley called, almost charging into the room.

Jumping, all four of us laughed.

Helissa got up and waved to the teacher, hiding our table as she stood in front of it.

Isabel moved the salt and circled the location on the map. It wasn't far from us at all, although I couldn't quite make out the exact location.

Ignoring Helissa, Mrs Hinley fumbled with her bag as she shoved it on her desk. The wooden old-fashioned writing desk had thick chunky legs and several drawers. She probably had a bottle of whisky hiding in there, like in the school films that were so popular. Maybe we could sneak a swig or two, although, being eighteen, we were legally allowed to drink, so hiding it wasn't necessary. Well, if we didn't care about being expelled of course. Academy rules meant that no alcohol was allowed on the grounds. Magic and diminished mental capacity was a violent mix, one that could be pretty fun, too.

"I've never met an illusionist witch," Dracian said, running his hand over the back of my chair. "They've never allowed one in the academy before." He popped his head between me and Isabel, narrowing his gaze on my face. "You must be special, Magic Fingers."

"Of course I am. Why else would they let a witch, who isn't a real witch according to you, come to such an esteemed academy? Oh... maybe because we are real witches. And you... you need to overcompensate by getting everyone to love you before you even get here. What are you afraid of Dracian Dread? That everyone will find out-?"

"Dracian, my dear," Mrs Hinley called. "Please take a seat!"

Keeping his dark, incredibly mysterious, eyes on me, he hesitated before pulling away. Had he been searching for my soul or something? I highly doubted that he would find much there. Ever since he had killed my parents, I hadn't felt much... except when I bawled my eyes out for my parents. Not that it did any good, the void would never be filled.

His movements were jarred, his legs slow as he went back to his seat, glancing over his shoulder at me until his butt was on the chair. It had been close - too close. I didn't want to reveal my hand too early, I had to be careful.

"What was that about?" Isabel hissed as Helissa went up to Mrs Hinley.

We heard her say something about Toby, so she must have been making the teacher aware of her stolen familiar. Let's hope she didn't say anything about the location spell. We weren't allowed to practice magic anywhere and everywhere at the academy. Classes were for learning skills as investigative witches. Magic could be practiced outside the classroom, but there were strict rules on what kind. Location spells were most certainly prohibited.

"Why do they have such stupid rules about spells?"

Okay, so my hands were itching and my neck was hot. I had to avoid Isabel's question, especially since my best friend knew me way too well. How could I tell her that I planned to out one of her friends as a murderer?

Allowing my change of subject, Isabel checked her phone, yet again. She was probably seeing if anyone had posted anything in the yearly Facebook group. I mean, really? A Facebook group for the first year kids? It was the lamest thing ever...

except when I might need to spy on Dracian's online activity. Hmm, maybe joining it would be a good thing after all.

"You know that we're limited because this amount of awesomeness..." She waved her hand around her head, winking as she flicked her hair behind her ear. "... would create a shit-ton of explosive magic. I mean, hundreds of witch students in one place, all learning about how to track and locate criminals? They're cray-cray."

"Did you-? I mean, what was that?"

Laughing, we shook our heads as Helissa joined us, a tear tracking down her cheek.

Sobering, we both looked between her and Mrs Hinley, who went to the chalkboard – yes, she lived in the dark ages – and wrote her name on it.

"She said that I have to wait for Professor Seaton to start his investigation before I do anything."

Taking her hand in mine, but quickly dropping it when her eyes went wide, I stuttered a response.

"We won't wait, we'll find him by ourselves. Can you...? I mean..." Swallowing, I glanced at Mrs Hinley, who was chattering on about who she was, blah, blah. "... Can you still *feel* him?"

Helissa's eyes widened before she nodded fast, her hand on her heart as she gripped the table. "Yes, he's still alive."

"Girls?" Mrs Hinley called. "I know this isn't high school, but you're still required to listen when I talk, which I can do a lot, I'll admit, but still..."

"Sorry," we all murmured, trying not to laugh.

It really was like being back at school. I had been free for a couple of months, but now I was in the confines of a place where restrictions were the norm. Just like my foster home. Why had I come to the academy again?

Glancing over at Dracian, I quickly looked away when he turned to stare at me. His dark eyes were delving still, trying to find out what I had meant, although I was pretty sure the killer boy wouldn't be intuitive enough to know that I'd seen him outside our house that night.

"We have a very special student with us this year." Mrs Hinley pointed at me, her long fingernail glistening pink as it reflected the dim lights that shone from their rustic metal chandeliers. The candles had been replaced with LED fake lights, carved in the exact style of the medieval candles. Wait, wasn't this a magical place, surely real wax would've been more fitting?

"Can you stop contemplating the ceiling, child, and come up here, please?"

Wringing my hands together, I swallowed as I slowly pushed back my chair and got to my feet.

The whole class watched me, boys and girls, their gazes boring into the witch who had been called to the front. It was a nightmare when watching it on films, but to be eighteen years old and summoned to be a spectacle, it almost made me want to vomit. Yes, I was still human. Well, sort of, not really.

"This little witch had the audacity to ignore me yesterday," Mrs Hinley said, a smile coming to her face when my gaze sought hers. "But, luckily, she saved the day."

I wasn't sure whether to be pleased that the teacher clearly had a grievance with the way I had acted - pleasing those above me had never been in my nature, except for my parents, of course. Although, I knew I had to behave. Underneath all my bravado, if it could be called that, I wanted to do well with my life once I had got my revenge.

"Alishia Jones is an illusionist witch with a difference." Reaching up to put a hand on my shoulder, Mrs Hinley squeezed, her pretty nails glowing bright against my black leather jacket. "Do you want to explain what it is you've managed to do?"

Licking my lips, I looked out to the class, keeping my head held high. My heart was literally playing my ribs like a drum, all panicky and shit. It wasn't a good feeling, not at all. I had never wanted to be famous, but if I wanted to survive a whole three years at the academy, I had to play the part. My ability was my ticket to a better life, one where I wasn't confined to the rules of others. First, my coven had kicked my family out, then I had lost my parents, only to go into a foster family who didn't give two craps about me, and now... at least I wasn't at the institute. I would never bow to that power, ever.

"My name is Alishia Jones, and I'm a magic-aholic."

Laughter bubbled across the room. I kept my gaze off Dracian, knowing full well that he would distract me with his haunting gaze. No one could see who I really was, the illusion was real. It had to be.

"When I was a child, I got so frustrated with not having my own magic, I began taking it from my friend." Smiling at Isabel, I almost dropped my gaze as a wash of memories flashed through my mind. "With her consent, of course."

Eyes stared at me, all fifteen students completely focused on the strange witch. I must have been a marvel to them, someone who didn't have a coven was unheard of, especially in normal society. Most witches in the room would have had their tuition paid for by their parents. Some of us were on scholarships. Every person in the room, bar me, had a coven, that much I knew.

Taking a deep breath, I cleared my throat. It was becoming extremely hot, and the staring did not help me feel confident or comfortable. Images of my parents made me almost cough.

"Go on, dear, we'd all love to hear your story. It's a special one!" Mrs Hinley was smiling warmly, encouragingly.

Digging deep, I shoved my memories away and held my jaw tight as I went on. "When my parents found out, they vowed to help me learn how to control my power. You see, everyone believes that we have no power, but in taking yours... that's our magic. Can humans take magic from witches? No. So why are we seen as less than a witch when we can drain you of-?"

"Okay," Mrs Hinley cut me off. "Tell us about your amazing invention."

"I wouldn't call it an invention. An invention is usually an object, but I can't really invent something using invisible matter."

Waving me on, Mrs Hinley narrowed her gaze at me. "Someone has learnt some science, I see. Well, my dear, you know very well what I mean."

Her pink cheeks were a warning sign. If I wanted to keep my head down at the academy, it probably wasn't a good idea to antagonise the teacher within the first five minutes. My bad.

"My father tested me, trying to find the science in how I took magic from other witches. He got me to visualise pulling magic from him when I touched his arm. He recorded the time it took until the magic stopped flowing and noted down what he felt too. Eventually, all I had to do was touch someone who had magic and it would automatically come, without me having to visualise."

Mouths dropped open, chairs shifted as the witches in the room grew uncomfortable. Er, maybe it hadn't been such a good idea to tell them about my little trick. If their expressions were anything to go by, they would stay at a 300 yard distance away from me at all times. I was used to it, so it wouldn't bother me. Much.

"Obviously, this is a dangerous skill to have, so my father decided to experiment. We worked together to use electric and life force from normal living creatures."

A gasp resounded around the room. A smile came to my lips as they started to whisper, their shocked faces almost making me laugh. The academy knew my story, and yet, they had still coveted me, just like all the other academies and the institute.

"Did you harm them?" Dracian called, his deep voice dripping with sweetness.

I half expected him to have a hand on his chest and the look of outrage scrawled across his features, but I was wrong. He looked fascinated, watching my every move, leaning forward on the desk and absorbing everything I said.

Shaking my head, I bit my lip hard. "No, of course not. We started with rats, just touching them gently. I realised quickly that I could do it, but I didn't like the idea of taking life force."

Crap, why had I told them about the life force? I never used the skill anyway, preferring to stick to electrical energy to make magic. They were literally staring at me as if I was a teen serial killer, ready to drain animals, people and witches of their magic. Good job, Alishia, way to frighten every person in your class within five minutes of being enrolled in the academy.

"Erm, so we know you don't do that." Mrs Hinley took a step back as she spoke, gesturing to the class. "Tell us why the academy personally invited you to attend."

"Basically," I said, getting rather frustrated at the bloody woman who had encouraged me to share my story. "I trained myself to touch electrical items to steal the magnetic pulse from them. That has helped me to gain magic without having to touch anyone. So, don't panic, I'm not about to creep into your room at night and..."

The frightened faces mixed with hard swallows made me panic, let alone them. Smiling, I laughed awkwardly when someone put their hand up and asked if they could be excused. Surely she wouldn't go and report me? I couldn't be chucked out on the first day, I had to avenge my parents and-

"No, we've only just started the class, you can wait until Alishia has finished." Mrs Hinley wiggled her finger.

My palms were so slick, I fumbled with my phone when I dug it out of my pocket.

Taking the small amount of energy before I could think, I breathed hard, my lungs working overtime to try and calm my nerves.

"Are you going to show us a picture of the animals you harmed?" someone asked.

Without waiting, I imagined the LED candles above us brightly aflame. The illusion appeared instantly, a spark crackling from the chandelier, catching everyone's attention. They gasped and screamed as flames burst from the candles, flickering high enough to lick the ceiling.

"Everyone, outside!" Mrs Hinley called. "Someone press the fire alarm!"

Students darted from their seats, staring up as they filtered out of the room, running to get away from the fire.

I ducked my head, following Isabel as she grabbed my hand and pulled me through the door.

"How did that happen?" a student asked Mrs Hinley.

Waving a hand towards me, another student screwed up his face. "It was probably a warning to stay away from her."

The scowl that rose up my chest was audible when everyone turned to look at me, backing away slightly. Good, let them be scared. If they stayed away from me, I could get on with what I needed to do.

"You're all fools!" Dracian Dread said, a smirk on his face as he came to stand beside me. "I think our friend was giving us a demonstration of her power."

"She was?" Mrs Hinley looked at me, a frown pulling her blonde eyebrows low. "Really, Alishia!"

The whining bell of the fire alarm resounded around us as the students stared at me, their mouths hanging open again.

Glancing at Dracian, I nodded.

"My name is Alishia Jones, and I'm an illusionist witch."

5

"I wrote the location down. It's a bar next to the grounds of the academy," Isabel said, pulling out the map.

We were on the grass outside the front of the building.

Professor Seaton had asked Mrs Hinley what had occurred in the classroom, but she had said it was a false alarm, not going into detail. It showed a loyalty I didn't deserve, not when I had tricked her and the class. However, I would take it. And try to run with it. When I saw her next, I would thank her for covering for me.

"You were so lucky to get away with that," Helissa said, spreading the map on the ground. "When Seaton stormed into the room after the alarm had been turned off, I almost crapped my pants for you."

"I'm surprised none of the students piped up." Taking a bite of my doughnut, I frowned when Isabel's face suddenly hovered close to mine. "Errr... yes?"

"That doughnut looks delicious. I'm trying not to gorge while I'm here, so I'm just going to sniff it if that's okay."

Pushing her slowly and gently away, I shook my head. "I don't want your snot particles near my sweet, sweet, delicious doughnut, woman. Stop giving in to societies rules of what you can and can't eat."

Her resolve lasted the whole of two seconds. Grabbing the doughnut out of my hand, she bit into the other side, closing her eyes and moaning rather embarrassingly loud.

"Sounds like you've found some food porn," a deep voice said behind us.

Tingles shot down my spine as Dracian crouched next to me, his expression friendly as he smiled at Isabel. I stared at my friend, refusing to look at the boy who just wouldn't leave us alone for one moment. We had promised Helissa that we would skip the afternoon class - it was only potions, which wasn't any of our speciality - to go and hunt out clues to find Toby.

"Doughnuts are much higher class than food porn," Isabel told Dracian as she flicked her silky, dark hair behind her shoulder. "They're food royalty. A classic erotic story."

"Wait, what? Are we...? I..."

Chuckling, Dracian put a hand on my shoulder, causing me to instantly tense up. "Don't worry, Vanilla Ice," he said in my ear. "I'm sure there's an ice cream truck around here somewhere, selling your favourite flavour."

"Don't be mean!" Helissa glared at the witch, who stood up, his hands held up in surrender.

"I'm only playing." Glancing at me, he raised his eyebrows. "See you later, guys."

Turning away, he joined two of his friends, who were standing nearby, looking bored.

My skin was literally itching, every part feeling the stench of his energy where he had touched me. Had he tried to intimidate me on purpose? Did he know my secret?

"Let's go."

All of us surged from the ground, discarding the remainder of our lunch in biodegradable bags.

Isabel shoved our very healthy food packaging in the bin as we passed, tapping it with one finger to spell it to the green compost heap in the gardens behind the academy. That witch was all about keeping Mother Earth clean. In a way, I did everything I could to support our mother, even though she had denied me magic from her dirt. Obviously, stealing electric probably wasn't as green as some people would think. Hey, at least I wasn't harming people.

"I've circled a building on the map. It's just over there," Isabel said, pointing through the bars of the gate.

Squinting, I grabbed the map off her and checked. "That's the Rose and Crown, where I work."

"You work there?" Isabel frowned at me. "How have you got a job in less than twenty four hours?"

"Girls!" Mrs Hinley's shout came from somewhere up high.

I could just imagine her blonde hair piled on top of her head as it hung out of one of the windows, her eyes glaring in our direction.

"Don't turn around," Helissa hissed. "Run!"

Following her lead, we picked up our pace, laughing when our rushing footsteps made other students stare at us.

Okay, so bunking class on the first day of school wasn't the ideal situation, but Toby had to be found. Professor Seaton would have a heart attack, well, maybe not, he was still pretty young, but anyway, he wouldn't be best pleased that we had started our own investigation.

The air rushed through my hair, flicking a blonde strand in front of my face. It went into my mouth as I opened it, ready to instruct the others on where to go. Almost choking, I laughed as I spat it out, suddenly feeling freer than I had for a very long time. My foster carers had kept me almost imprisoned the last five years, threatening to call the institute if I dared to do anything against their will.

"This way," Isabel called, smiling at me as her long silky hair flew behind her.

Ducking around the entrance, we left the grounds of the academy and sprinted towards the bar.

It was strange that the location spell had taken us to the place where I had just got a job. It had been barely twenty four hours since I had been trained in how to pull a pint, and yet, I was returning.

Slowing down, I came to a stop, bending over to catch my breath.

Isabel jogged on the spot, her gaze tracing the area around the pub. It was fairly quiet, most people having gone back to work or the academy after lunch.

"You need to get to the gym," my friend said, clapping me on the back.

Glancing at Helissa, I raised my eyebrows. The other witch shook her head, also struggling with her breath. Good, she could be my backup best friend for moments like this. Although, that was unkind, I shouldn't think of her as a backup. Plus, I barely knew

101

her, she could actually be extremely annoying, even if she had clicked with us quickly. I hadn't even stopped to consider why I was going to so much effort to help her.

"Are you that type of person?" I pointed my thumb at Isabel.

"You've got to be kidding," Helissa said, cringing as she stretched her back. "I read books, I play Fortnite religiously and then I sleep. A girl needs nothing more."

"Fortnite?" Isabel got out her phone and snapped a selfie with us panting and huffing in the background.

"Let me guess," I said, trying to snatch the phone out of her hand. "The caption will be.... *Winning the race like...*"

Laughter erupted from my friend as she flung her arm around me and pushed me at the same time. Indicating the pub, she tucked her phone away and clucked her tongue against the roof of her mouth. "Let's go and find Toby, losers."

Helissa trailed behind, her face almost crumbling in on itself as she was reminded of why we were currently breaking all the rules of the academy. Was it really that heart-breaking to lose a familiar? My parents had let me have a cat, well, for a while, anyway. When they realised I could drain any living creature, not that I had ever completely drained anything, they gave the cat to Isabel. Boy, my parents were crueller than I had realised in that moment. A squeeze of my chest reminded me how painful that was. If it was bad enough for me, Helissa must have been feeling despair.

Moving away from Isabel, who got her phone out yet again, I went back to Helissa. "We will find him!" I told her, putting my hand on her shoulder.

Quickly pulling away, I apologised, my cheeks flaring red. Without saying anything, the witch with the famous name grabbed my hand and held tight before letting go.

"I'm not afraid of you." Smiling, she followed Isabel through the door and into the bar.

A rush of weirdness ran over me. I had a job in this establishment, and yet, I had no idea how to approach my new boss who stood behind the bar reserved for humans.

"It's so frustrating that humans aren't allowed to know about us." Isabel sighed as she stared at a boy who played pool with his friends. "I'd like to play pool with him."

"Hello, Alishia," Frankie greeted, waving me through. "You're keen!"

We ducked through the bar, following him through the door around the back and into the other bar. "You do know that you can use the magic entrance, don't you?"

"Ah, yeah," I said, trying not to search the room with my gaze as he gestured for us to go around to the main area of the bar. "I know I don't officially start for a few days, but we're here for social reasons. Sort of."

"Sort of?"

Pouring us Cokes when Helissa requested our drinks, he frowned at me, his bushy eyebrows pulled low over his grey eyes. His tummy protruded from his jeans, a slight overhang telling a story of lonely nights sipping on beer. Although, an image flashed through my mind of Frankie the barman, partying hard. Hhmmm... he didn't seem the type.

Isabel stared at me, her eyes stretched wide. "Oh, this is my new boss, Frankie. Frankie, these are my friends."

The girls studied him, analysing the bar manager who stood with his hands on his hips. Something about his energy had warmed me to him straight away. Maybe his being an illusionist witch helped me to trust him. And yet, the others ducked their gaze before looking at me. Should I ask Frankie about the snake? Or was it safer to try and scope out the place ourselves?

"Nice to meet you," the man said, bowing his head and pretending to doff his invisible hat... until a real top hat appeared, the black silk shining under the lamps above.

"What sort of clientele do you get in here?" Helissa asked, taking the decision out of my hands.

When the hat crumbled into nothing, Isabel sat forward. "You're an illusionist witch, too!"

Putting his finger to his mouth, he smiled as he shushed her. "Don't tell everyone. My punters would be distraught if they found out that I hadn't really seen the 1966 World Cup final."

Pointing at a picture of him with the winning England squad, he wiggled his eyebrows.

I rolled my eyes, wondering why the hell he would use what little power he had to cast such an old-fashioned illusion. Anyone could photoshop the same image nowadays, it wasn't exactly hard.

"My clientele, as you so elegantly put it," he said, wiping the waxed wooden bar absentmindedly, "...is usually students. A few witches from outside the academy wander in occasionally. Oh, and there's a group of warlocks who play pool on a Saturday night. Why do you ask?"

Watching the man go through the motions, I tried not to snatch the dirty cloth from his hand. Witches were reviled for doing menial jobs. Why waste their magic? However, illusionist witches were expected to be at the bottom of the cesspool of magical beings, considering they were classed as un-magical. I would never be like Frankie, wasting away in a bar.

A flash of guilt squeezed my chest as he glanced around his establishment, a satisfied smile coming to his lips. Just because I couldn't be cooped up in the same pub day in, day out, didn't mean he wasn't happy. It didn't make him less than a man. My parents had taught me to be kind, to not assume something about a person, and here I was, forgetting their lessons.

Helissa leant forward, her gaze searching his. "Have you heard anything about a snake in the last twenty four hours?"

Frowning, Frankie nodded slowly. "Yes. In fact..." Going over to the till to serve a straggly student who stood at the bar, he pointed towards the door. "... a young lad offered me a snake just two hours ago. Said I could have it for cheap."

"What?" Helissa spat as the student watched us.

"A snake?" he said, his gaze skimming across my face and quickly dismissing me.

He could probably feel that I had no magic in me. All witches could feel magic from one another. When they came into contact with a warlock, their energy was different, so it was obvious what they were. A ton of people were confused as to the old tales of witches and warlocks. Back in the good old days, which felt like millennia to me, witches were female, warlocks were male. However, with the decline of warlocks and their evil ways, a new race was born. Male witches started to be born without the distinct magic of warlocks. They were not able to form physical magic, unlike their old male ancestors. They were suddenly able to cast spells as well as any female witch, using herbs, chants and tarot cards. They had always been able to do the witch magic to some degree, but with the loss of their physical magic, their power in witch magic increased.

"What can I get you?" Frankie asked the student as Helissa and Isabel turned to me.

Lowering her voice, Helissa spoke urgently. "If he was in here two hours ago, he might still be close by. Maybe we could do another location spell and head straight there?"

"That might be a good idea. You go and start that, I'll get more info from Frankie."

"Can you trust him?" Isabel said, twirling a strand of hair around the tip of her finger.

Glancing at the barman, I tilted my head to the side. "He gave me a job instantly, without knowing who I was. Plus, we have something in common."

"You trust him because he's like you, but is that enough?" Helissa took my hand when I frowned. "Think like an investigator."

Nodding, I gently pulled my hand away when my fingers tingled. She was consciously giving me her magic, but I didn't like it. Not one bit. It was kind that they weren't afraid to touch me. In fact, a lump swelled to my throat. Bloody hell, what was it with the kind witch of the west wing? The academy goody two shoes? The one who made me want to cry right this moment? Why couldn't she live up to the nastiness of her ancestors? Ugh, she was just a nice girl, and I had to get used to her being nice to me.

"I won't tell him why we're looking for a snake. I've got the perfect alibi."

"Alibi?" Isabel said, her perfectly plucked eyebrows raised. "Do you know what that is?"

Shrugging, I indicated that they take the map to the corner booth. "Just... go and do it, I'll get my investigator head on."

"Dudette..." Placing a hand on my arm, Isabel gave me a woeful look. "An alibi is when you have proof that you weren't in a particular place, at a particular time, usually doing a particular criminal activity. I don't think you've got one of those."

Oh yeah, I knew that. And they allowed me into the academy, why?

Leaving me sitting at the bar, the others took their drinks and settled in the booth.

Frankie finished serving the student, who slowly took off his academy blazer and sat nearby, before coming back to me.

"We're doing an assignment," I told my new boss as he handed me a small pile of paperwork. Skimming the words, I put the application form into my bag as I continued. "We have to investigate the disappearance of a snake, stolen from one of the dorms."

"Make sure you fill that out before your first shift. Just because I'm a witch, doesn't mean I don't have to please the human government with official employment records." Frankie checked around the bar, his gaze lingering on the student who pretended to read something on his phone.

My voice was low, hopefully too low for the student to hear. Although, I could see his ears pricking, trying to listen. He would know what was happening at the academy.

There had already been a post on Facebook from one of the popular girls asking students to keep an eye out for Helissa's familiar.

"I promise. So, can you tell me more about the man who... you know...?" Widening my eyes, I nodded my head sideways at the intruder.

Frankie understood, a slight nod telling me that he would keep his voice to a minimum. "The snake-"

Reaching over as his voice carried much louder than I expected, I grabbed hold of the second till that was to my left. Pulling on the electrical current, I threw up a muffling illusion spell. The student nearby glanced at me before looking back at his phone. He wouldn't be able to hear our exact words, instead a banal conversation would put him off track. I had made sure to add a sprinkle of tinnitus to the illusion, which was obviously working because he started to shake his head.

113

"Right, he can't hear us now. You don't do subtle well, considering you run an illegal bar for supernaturals, do you?"

Narrowing his gaze on the till before looking at the boy, Frankie opened and closed his mouth. "How did you just do that? You didn't... I mean, did you...?"

"My friend held my hand a moment ago, giving me a bit of her magic. We're training to be undercover agents, we need to act as if we already are."

Shrugging, I took out a notebook from my bag and clicked on my pen. Hopefully, I embodied an efficient agent. Although, it was highly unlikely with the leather jacket and printed school skirt. It was beyond heinous that the academy made us wear a uniform. How were we supposed to look official?

Shaking my head out of my own incredibly silly thoughts, I cleared my throat. "Please, can you tell me what the man said? Did you see the snake?"

Leaning his hand on the bar, he looked up as he thought. "No, I didn't see the snake. He showed me a bag, said it would help me with my magic. Come to think of it, it didn't click before. He said that he knew how much I liked casting illusions. Which means he must know me."

Doodling a bum, I smiled to myself as I added a dimple, completely unaware that Frankie watched me until he cleared his throat.

"Very professional."

Mumbling an incoherent reply, I quickly scribbled what he'd said. So, the person had been in the bar before, a regular perhaps?

"Did you know the man? Has he been in before?"

Glancing over at the girls, I checked that they were on task. They were. Good, we would solve the case in no time. I didn't know who I thought I was... Velma from

Scooby Doo or something. Glasses would probably suit me-

"I've seen his face a few times, yes. I don't know him, though. Blonde hair, similar colour to yours. I'm sure he's a student at the academy." Clicking his fingers, Frankie turned and flipped over a board that had, just moments before, looked like a mirror at the back of the bar. Behind it, CCTV cameras played scenes from both the human bar and the paranormal.

"Huh," I said, leaning my head to the side. "That's what you call an illusionist jackpot!"

How had I not been able to notice his illusion? And how was he keeping the illusion up? Usually, most illusionist witches quickly ran out of the magic they had stolen. If I didn't top up with electric, I even ran out.

"Let me rewind quickly, just keep your enquiring friend busy." Nodding at the boy who kept glancing at me, he pressed a few buttons and got to work.

Our gaze met, the young boy raising his eyebrows in greeting. He would be hearing a completely different conversation while the illusion put Frankie still standing right in front of me. All I had to do was imagine it and it was so. A few of my witch friends in junior school had wished that they were able to cast the same magic, but they'd quickly changed their mind when I was chucked out of the coven. Bastards.

"Did you say you were looking for a snake a moment ago?" The boy stared at me, his face watching my every move.

"I did."

He must have heard my mention of the snake before I'd cast the illusion. Nil Points to Alishia for not doing the spell in time.

Inclining his head towards the door, the boy blinked slowly. "Some dude just asked me to buy a snake off him. He's right outside."

Crapping hell. My heart jumped into my throat as Frankie turned at the boy's words. If the person who had been in the bar two hours ago was still here, was he waiting for someone? Surely, if he just wanted to sell the snake to get it out of the way, he would've taken it to a pet shop.

"You better get out there," Frankie said. "You could fail your *assignment* if you don't catch him."

Alarm bells rung in my mind. Were they tricking me? How did I know that the pair of them weren't setting me up? I didn't know either of them, and even though Frankie was an illusionist witch, his power now scared me. I had never met another illusionist witch who had managed to fool me.

"Thanks," I said to them as I got up from my seat.

The girls came over, grabbing my arm and propelling me away. I glanced at Frankie, who mouthed a Good Luck, before hiding his CCTV cameras.

"The location spell showed that he was here still," Isabel said.

"So, I listened in to your conversation," Helissa whispered, dragging me across the floor, past the pool table, and to the door. "Let's get the bastard who stole my Toby."

"Wait!"

My protest was ignored as the others shoved me outside. The bright light of the sun glared straight in my face, blinding me. When I looked away, I spotted a boy sitting on a bench. He had surged to his feet when we had appeared, his expression hopeful.

When he saw that it was us, he swallowed hard, grabbed the bag next to him and made a run for it. The walkway was cobblestoned, with a metal fence encasing the grounds of the academy behind it. Benches lined the pretty pathway, one end leading to the main entrance of my new school, the other led into the parkland that surrounded the back of it.

The boy ran towards the parkland, his feet super quick. He must have known who we were, which made him the prime suspect. Oh, I liked playing detective.

"That's him!" Helissa shouted.

She was the one who had caught him kidnapping, no wait, snake-napping Toby, she could probably recognise his magic.

Thrusting into action, we set off after him. Two lots of running in one day, I would be able to do a marathon in no time, except, I was still tired from our earlier escape. My legs ran as fast as they could, but we were no match for the boy. His sprint took him out of the walkway and into the woods beyond.

"Cast a spell!" I panted, only just keeping an eye on his jacket as it flapped out behind him.

Helissa huffed a freezing spell, throwing her hand out. The boy tripped, his body skidding to the green grass.

We were almost on him when he turned, glaring at us. "He made me do it!"

Before we could reach him, he puffed into thin air. Transportation spells were only used by advanced witches and were only taught at academies by ley line witches. How had the boy been able to whisk himself and Toby away?

"Shit!" I barked, apologising to an elderly lady as she meandered out from behind a tree.

We stayed quiet, catching our breath as she moved past, glaring at us with one of those annoying stares that only old ladies could give. It instantly made me feel guilty of a crime I didn't commit.

"I can't believe he got away," I spat, taking my phone out when it burst into noise.

121

Wait, what the hell was my foster mother doing calling me? Surely, she had realised that I wanted nothing to do with her. Letting it ring off, I faced the others.

"How did that happen? Why didn't one of you cast a spell earlier? You could've tripped him or at least managed to get his bag off him. If Toby-"

"Calm down," Isabel said, frowning at me. "We saw his face, which means it will be a lot easier to find him now."

"Aghh!" Clenching my hands into fists, I spun as I growled, tempted to punch the tree trunk near me.

The others stared at me, I could feel their gazes burning into my back. I ignored them, sucking in a breath, slow and calm, just like the therapist had taught me after I had lost my parents.

Not only had we lost the person responsible for snake-napping Toby, my foster mother had chosen that moment to

122

remind me of what I had run from only the day before. My life sucked balls.

"It's fine." Helissa came and stood right in front of me. "We will catch him, I'm sure of it. He definitely had Toby, I could feel him."

Sucking my bottom lip into my mouth, I nodded, unable to speak as tears came to my eyes. What was wrong with me? Why was I so upset about a snake? Although, he wasn't just a snake, he was someone's familiar.

The fact that she could feel him showed me how close they were. I hadn't been that close to anyone or anything for... well, for five years. If I dared to allow myself to care for anyone, they could be ripped away from me at any time.

"Let's get back to the academy. Professor Seaton might not help us now that we've skipped class." Nudging me, Helissa smiled sadly, indicating that we head back down the pathway. I followed, silent as Isabel chatted away to me, trying to get me to talk. She

123

spoke of the past, reminding me of the things we got up to. I could tell that she thought recalling the memories would cheer me up, but it just reminded me of what I had lost even more.

My mother had always told me that every phase in life had a lesson to show me. I hadn't reacted so strongly to anything for a long while, able to control my temper. What had triggered me so violently?

"Do you remember Misty?" Isabel whispered, her eyes welling up as we approached the school gates.

Swallowing ten thousand times, I cursed my friend in my head. Maybe it had been better not being around her all this time. Even her gorgeous face reminded me of a time that I'd buried, a time when I had allowed myself to be open.

Not anymore. I had vowed to destroy the person who had destroyed me, and I would never allow myself to soften, ever again.

6

"I'll meet you there," I told Helissa as I left the bedroom.

My new roommate hadn't rested well, her fitful sleep keeping me awake most of the night too. Professor Seaton had been as useless as a chocolate teabag... or teacup... I could never remember the saying my mother had often used, but I liked to try, just to keep a part of her close to me.

The door closed quietly behind me, the click shutting out my new friend's anxious face. A flutter of white caught my eye, making me frown. A piece of paper had been stuck to the door. Ripping it off, I dropped it as the magic that had laced the hands of whoever had posted it sank into me.

"Eww…"

Bending in the empty hallway, I pulled my sleeve over my hand and picked the note up again. My gaze traced the writing, my eyes stretching wide when the words sunk in.

If you want the snake returned, Alishia Jones must give up her secret to her illusion magic. If not, the snake will be killed and the academy blown up. You have three days to write it down and send it to Snake through Infinity.

Infinity? The students had mentioned something about Infinity. Apparently, it was the academy's secret postal service. Students could send private letters or assignments without anyone being able to read them. It helped with the risk of copying work,

126

especially when it was sensitive information regarding criminal case studies.

"Miss Alishia Jones." Dracian's deep voice travelled down my spine and back up, the dulcet tones making me shiver.

He was coming out of his room on the opposite side of the hall.

Tucking the note in my pocket, I cleared my throat and turned to greet him. I couldn't exactly pretend I hadn't heard him. Playing deaf wasn't right, especially when he had probably seen me stiffen. He must have been able to tell how his voice made me melt... wait, no, not melt, he was...

"Did Professor Seaton help your friend?"

... annoyingly hot and apparently caring. Ugh!

"Not really," I replied, telling myself that the reason my heart was beating like a bloody drum was because of the note, not because of Dracian Dread, the one boy I hated more than anyone. "He had someone come into the room to cast an energy spell. They reckon the snake-napper-"

"Snake-napper? That's what they're calling him, is it?" The twitch of his lip made my eyes narrow on him as he stepped closer.

"Well," I muttered, dropping my gaze. "That's what I'm calling him."

My eyes rose as his leather boots, which were tucked under blue jeans, came into view. His black T-shirt was pulled tight over muscles that shouldn't have belonged to an eighteen year old, especially not one who had used them to kill my parents. The blood that had lined my kitchen floor had been bright red. The same colour was splashed across Dracian's T-shirt, hidden under his blazer, used to create an image of - was that a picture of a werewolf? I mean, really?

"What did they find?"

Lifting my face, I looked into his eyes, trying my hardest not to lunge at him. No, not to kiss him, but to kill him.

128

I had found them, my parents, sprawled, face down, in their own blood. Someone had conjured a spell to kill them, squeezing the blood vessels in their brains so hard, they... they...

"Are you okay? You look a bit pale." Reaching for me, he paused when I jumped back, scowling at him.

Not bothering to reply, I spun around him, storming down the hall to the stairs. Before I turned out of the hallway, I glanced over my shoulder. He watched me, his dark eyes brooding under a frown. Yes, Mr Dread, you keep looking puzzled. The longer you're unaware of what I know, the easier it will be for me to take you down.

My footsteps were silent on the stone steps as I took them two at a time. Tears blurred my vision as I shoved the image of my parents from my head. Five years ago, I had come downstairs from an incredible nights sleep to the worst nightmare any thirteen year old girl had to endure. Well, any person, regardless of age. It had broken me, and I had barely pieced myself back together.

"Just be careful," I heard a female whisper as the clatter of high heels sounded below.

Looking over the balcony, I spotted Mrs Hinley and Professor Seaton going into the entrance hall.

Skipping faster, I came to the bottom of the stairs, just as their voices disappeared through the doorway and into the ballroom.

When the Professor had come to our room last night, he hadn't said a word about our absence from afternoon sessions. Either, he didn't know, or he chose to ignore it, considering that it probably wouldn't look great on the academy that a crime had been committed as soon as the school term had begun.

Who would've thought? An academy that taught witches how to be undercover agents not able to solve a crime within its very own walls. What would the world say?

"Don't overthink it, Janine," the professor said. "We'll find the person who took Toby. I'm sure it was just... I dunno, a misunderstanding."

Seriously?

"Seriously?" Mrs Hinley laughed, the sound echoing in the huge room as I tiptoed closer to the entrance and hid in the shadows beside the door.

It was dawn. First class wasn't for another hour, but I had wanted to get a head start on the day. I had told Helissa that I wanted to shower, but I had done that the night before, just so I was ready for the morning. My mother had always taught me to be prepared, so I was going to the library to read over the lesson we had missed on potions. Not that reading the words would do any good, I couldn't make potions, even if I wanted to. It was forbidden for illusionist witches to practice herbology and anything that used physical matter to create spells.

"We don't have time for this. The school year has just begun and already we've had three major issues." Professor Seaton's voice was hushed, his tone tense.

Three issues? Something else must have happened already. Although, the incident on the balcony hadn't been mentioned on the first day, not in class anyway.

Without thinking, I reached into my pocket and took the note out again. Light shone down from the orbs, the colour red nearest to me, casting a ray over the words scribbled on the page. I hadn't even had time to take a dump, let alone process everything that had happened in the last two days. What would I do with the note?

"I'm sure they're not connected." Mrs Hinley's heels clicked a couple of times before it went quiet. "Just be patient and allow the students to settle. We do need to investigate the case of the snake, but a second girl almost losing all her magic in the first day of class cannot get out."

Losing her magic? What? How was that even possible? I had wondered if the girl who'd had a seizure on the first day had been electrocuted through me. I had even asked Mrs Hinley how she was doing. She had assured me that she was well again. How could a second student be almost drained?

Now, my mind rattled with thoughts as the sound of lips smacking in the room made me frown. Leaning forward, I held my hair back as I peeked around the edge of the door. Ermmm... I wasn't sure if my eyes were deceiving me, considering, you know, Mrs Hinley's name started with a Mrs, but I was pretty sure Professor Seaton wasn't Mr Hinley. And, I was even surer that the sound of smacking lips wasn't the pair enjoying tea and cake together... no, they were in a clandestine embrace, their lips locked tight.

Pulling away from the professor, Mrs Hinley let go of him, her head whipping around to check the entrance to the ballroom. Darting back just before her gaze landed on me, I swallowed hard. Had she seen me watching them like a pervert?

"Tell me more about the girl. Did anything happen before she passed out?" Mrs Hinley sounded like the one in charge, not Professor Seaton.

Coughing, the professor answered her in a strained voice. "Apparently, she had been in potions class, making a liquor for pain. Halfway through class, she asked to go to the restroom and never returned. The tutor sent her friend to find her." A shuffle was followed by the flick of a lighter. After an inhale, the professor went on. "She was found passed out on the bathroom floor. When taken to the infirmary, the nurse confirmed that her magic had gone, she was almost empty."

"Empty?" Mrs Hinley whispered loudly. "She could've died on the first day of school!"

If a witch was drained of their magic, they would die. It was their life-force, the thing keeping them alive. Unlike me, who had no real magic, I would die like a human did, of old age and shit. Hopefully. I didn't want to live fast and die young, it wasn't my motto.

"Was Alishia Jones in the class?" Mrs Hinley's voice shook as I gasped a breath, trying to stay silent.

Why would she ask if I was present? Surely, they didn't suspect me? Would they really think that I would be brash enough to come straight in and steal someone's magic on the first day? They had no idea who I was, just that I had something they wanted.

"No, she skipped class with her friends." The professor sighed. "Besides, she seems like a nice girl, even if she was involved in

135

the other two incidents. She's had a tough time, I'm not going to assume the worst."

Shuffling of feet made me take a few steps back from the door. "No, you're right, I shouldn't just blame the poor girl. She seemed very eager to help on the first day. Let's get our team onto the case, maybe the witch had come into contact with someone before she came into the academy."

A hummed affirmation accompanied their footsteps as they approached the door. I couldn't run, they would see me. Why had I stayed frozen to the spot? Just because my name was mentioned? Of course, they would blame the illusionist witch, it wasn't a surprise, but my chest squeezed hard anyway.

"The snake will be found," Professor Seaton said as they came closer.

Pushing myself into the wooden wall as much as I could, I touched my phone, pulling on the energy and draining the battery. Imagining myself as part of the wall, I held my breath as the teachers went past, not even turning to look in my direction. They marched across the entrance hall towards the classroom hallway.

"Of course it will," Mrs Hinley said. "Otherwise, our reputation as the best academy for training crime hunters will be ruined."

My breath rushed out of me as my stomach almost dropped to the floor. My magic had come in handy, but boy, it had been close. If they had caught me listening in, they would've instantly assumed that I was guilty. Why else would I be skulking in the hallway, listening to their conversation and perving at their kiss?

Shaking my head of the memory, I hurried across the floor, heading towards the steps that led to the platform above the entrance hall. The library beckoned me as I tripped up them, my heart still pounding hard.

Slowing when an instinct stronger than survival kicked in, I glanced over the stone bannister. A shadow moved in the corner of the entrance hall, near to the learning wing. Was that someone watching me? It sure felt like it. The dimness made me doubt myself. I was probably making it up in my head.

Laughing to myself, I clenched my hands and tried to shake the feeling that someone's gaze followed my every move. Turning my attention back to the note, I resumed my ascent up the steps.

What would I do with the note in my pocket? I wasn't about to send my secret out into the ether, straight into the hands of an unknown assailant. I hadn't banked on people being so interested in me and my gift. I was just plain old Alishia Jones, blonde hair, blue eyes, five foot seven wearing an Undercover Witch Academy green and navy checked skirt with a black leather jacket. See? So dull, so-

"Hello, Alishia."

As I came to the top of the steps, I almost tripped over. His voice had startled me, making me almost drop my backpack. It was the boy who had comforted Helissa when Toby was first taken.

"Hi, errr..."

"James."

"James."

"You're up early." Putting a book in his own bag, he watched me, his bright blue eyes appraising my figure. If he wasn't careful, I would poke his eye out with a... well, I didn't have anything but my finger. That would have to do. It was at times like this that I wished I had more magic. My battery would need charging before I could steal any more electricity and transform it into magic. Otherwise, I could have pulled an illusion of me being a teacher, not Alishia Jones.

"I missed a class yesterday-"

"I heard you skipped it." His eyebrows rose, a smile quirking his lips. "I don't blame you. I suppose an illusionist witch is too cool for potions."

Raising my own eyebrows, I crossed my arms over my chest. "What you mean to say is that I have no use of potions because I can't use them."

Shrugging, he shook his head. "You can think what you like, I mean what I say." Coming closer, he bent so his head was near my ear. "Or... do I?"

When his breath hit my earlobe, I shuddered. My intuition ran amok when boys were around. I couldn't read them at all. He had shown a ton of interest in Helissa on the night Toby had been taken, but I hadn't seen him since.

"If you need help finding the snake, let me know." Without looking at me, he trotted down the steps, his feet loud on the stone.

Pushing my way through the stained glass double doors, I entered the library and study hall. Rows of dark wooden bookshelves separated the library into sections. I almost squealed when I saw how many books there were. Illusionist witches were rarely allowed to read magic books. If a witch knew spells, they could cast them with their own magic, but an illusionist witch would have to steal it from somewhere else before they could conjure them.

That was why I had instantly assumed that James' words had an ulterior meaning. Not many witches encouraged our studying. I had heard of a few illusionist witches training to become investigators for the agencies, but they were always stuck behind a desk, never out in the field.

I wanted to be out in the field. After I had calmed yesterday, a rush of energy had lifted my spirits. The adrenaline had helped me to feel alive. Chasing the boy who had Toby had given me a reason to live. It was sad, that little old me had nothing to live for, but it was true.

"Are you just going to stand there?" the librarian asked as I stood, staring, lost in thought.

Smiling at the homely woman, I made my way to the corner where there were sofas and a coffee table. Taking out my book on potions, I opened it and laid it on the table. My hand brought out the note and placed it on top of the page.

They wanted my secret. Everyone. The professors, the institute, and even a random stranger, who would stoop very low to get it. Surely, they wouldn't kill Helissa's familiar?

If I gave up my secret, which wasn't really a hard secret, just practicing channelling electrical energy, I wouldn't be relevant anymore. I would probably be chucked out of the academy. I wasn't prepared to tell others how I did it. I just couldn't give that part of myself away, even to save a snake.

Did that make me a bitch?

7

Banging jolted me out of sleep. Who the hell wakes up so early in the morning? Oh yeah, I had the day before. But, that had worn off quickly.

Helissa jumped up from her bed, clasping her chest and falling to her knees. Her sob rent the air, forcing me up to my feet. Huh, that was a little dramatic, it was only someone at the door.

"What is it?" I asked her, putting my hand on her shoulder before remembering not to touch her.

Tears poured down her face as she clutched herself, unable to talk.

Isabel shouted from outside the room making me rush to the door.

When I opened it, I froze. Several students stood on the other side, their expressions full of concern.

"What's going on?" I almost shouted.

"It's Toby," Isabel said, thrusting into the room.

Looking down at my PJs when the others stared at me, I quickly shoved the door closed. What was wrong with unicorns? Just because I wanted to be one, didn't make me twelve.

Isabel joined Helissa on the floor, her arms instantly going around her. I couldn't quite clear my sleepy head. What was going on?

"I... what happened?"

Ignoring me, Isabel hugged Helissa tightly, almost cooing. My friend had done the same to me when we were thirteen, sitting in my living room, waiting for the coroner to take my parents' bodies away.

"Go to the ballroom, use your magic to cast an illusion," Isabel ordered me.

Taking out my clothes from the rickety wardrobe, I donned them quickly. Bending back into the wooden wardrobe, I crouched to access my bag. I hadn't shown anyone my power packet, which was basically a portable power generator. It was part of the secret that I was trying to hide. The pack was made of plastic, but the button released high voltage electricity when pushed. It would kill a normal person, but not me. If anyone knew I had it, the powers that be would confiscate it. The invention was too dangerous to not only other witches and humans, but to their rule. If illusionist witches could find a way permanently have magic, they would form their own covens. That would be extremely daunting to the institute.

"Get to it!" Isabel clutched Helissa to her, waving me away.

I didn't understand, why was I being dismissed? Pushing the button of my plastic gadget, I closed my eyes and allowed the electricity to filter into me, transmuting it to magic instantly.

Once full, I packed it away, quickly hurrying from the room.

There could only be one reason that Helissa was so cut up. Toby was dead.

My heart thumped as I rushed down the hallway, dodging the other students, who stood around, watching our door as if some miracle would emerge. Unfortunately, although I was pretty cool sometimes, I was no miracle.

"I found it," Dracian said, joining me as I jogged past him.

Blinking, I almost tripped, my legs turning to jelly. If he had found Toby, he was

147

instantly the prime suspect, I would make sure Helissa knew that.

Trying to take my arm, he let go when I frowned at him. "Don't touch me, remember?"

He fell back as I skipped down the steps, sneaking a quick look at him when I reached the bottom. He watched me, his dark eyes narrowed on my back. I couldn't help it, he had no right to touch me. Although, that hadn't really been why I snapped at him. No one was allowed to touch me, it was too dangerous.

"Alishia?" Mrs Hinley called as I approached the ballroom doors.

One stood open, revealing the crowd that had gathered in the room.

I paused as Mrs Hinley dashed out of the teaching wing. Her hair was a mess as she tugged at it, trying to make it sit on the top of her head. Her small frame swayed as her high heels made the most awful racket. Why did she have to wear the annoying stilettos? They made more noise than a plane going overhead.

"I need you," the teacher said, gripping the edge of my jacket and pulling me into the ballroom.

My eyes instantly lifted to where everyone was staring. A beautiful golden chandelier hung from the painted ceiling. The cherubs above poured water from their hands, straight onto the light fixture. A cascade of real water fell down the long metal rope holding the chandelier. The twinkling crystals looked liquescent as they reflected the light that streamed in from the floor to ceiling windows on either side of the room.

Hanging from one of the arms of the chandclier was Toby the snake. His body limp, blood dripping from his lifeless head.

"I need you to hide him." Mrs Hinley licked her lips as she glanced around, speaking quietly. "Your magic leaves no trace, so it won't affect the imprint of the killer."

Students whispered amongst themselves, their eyes wide as they pointed at the familiar.

Poor Helissa. No wonder she was in a lot of pain, her main source of magic had been severed. A familiar helped a witch ground her magic, creating a bond stronger than any other. I hadn't been jealous of that bond, no, not ever... not me. Bitches.

"I could hide him, but he still needs to be collected. It's not fair that he's dangling up there for everyone to see."

Nodding, Mrs Hinley put a hand to her chest. "You're right, of course. Parents are about to come in for the first quarterly coffee morning, so we'll hide him for now. Once they've arrived, we'll escort them out the back of the ballroom to the rose garden. Will you stay and get him down then? Professor Seaton will tell you what you need to note down before you touch him. This is a formal investigation now, my dear, your first one!"

I had never imagined that I would be on the job as soon as I walked through the academy doors. It was interesting that Mrs Hinley wanted me to use my magic to hide the snake because it didn't interfere with the magic already on him. Maybe an illusionist witch, namely me, could do well for herself as an agent after all.

"Okay, I'll do it. Can you call the students? Distract them while I make it look like he's not there."

Moving away from the teacher when she nodded, I circled around the outside of the gathered crowd. Several other teachers were intermingled with the students, not doing a very good job of drawing their attention away from the slaughtered familiar.

My mind slipped back to the note that was tucked into my jacket pocket. This was my fault, it had to be. Panic started to rise, making my hands shake as Mrs Hinley called for everyone's attention.

As soon as they all turned to her, I lifted my arm and whispered a cover spell, aiming it at Toby. My heart squeezed in my chest as he disappeared. Well, it looked like he did, I could still see him faintly, but others wouldn't be able to.

My first job was done, but the second... that would be hard. Helping to take down the familiar that had been murdered because of me didn't sit high on my feel good radar.

If the person who had threatened me was the same boy who had killed Toby, then they might indeed blow up the school. What did I do? Who could I trust? If I told Helissa and Isabel about the note, they would blame me for Toby's death. I wouldn't blame them, either, I blamed me. Ugh.

"Parents are just arriving for our introduction coffee morning. Once you've greeted them, please make your way to class!" Mrs Hinley called, dismissing them.

As they turned back to stare at the chandelier, some of them gasped. They couldn't see where the snake had gone, some even shook their heads and frowned.

Good, my spell had worked. At least I could save Helissa the embarrassment of the whole school staring at her poor familiar. It would make up for my mistake, right? Probably not, I had-

"Alishia?" a familiar voice shouted from the entrance hallway.

Freezing, I muttered an invisibility spell. There was only a small amount of magic left in me, but I used it to hide from them. Everyone else would be able to see me, which didn't bloody help. Hardly any of the students would know who I was, but there was a couple standing nearby who knew me from our classes.

The students watched as my foster mother and father stormed into the room, shouting loudly between themselves. They were obviously still pissed that I had done them over when I had run away from the institute. Maybe the institute had offered them a hefty sum for turning me over, although, I wasn't that much of a catch, so I didn't see the big deal.

"Alishia Jones?" the woman called, almost screeching. "I know you're in here, I saw you come in a moment ago!"

Swallowing, I backed away from the students. A couple looked in my direction, their eyebrows raised. I shook my head, putting a finger to my mouth. If the bastards ratted me out, I wouldn't forgive them. Surely, they wouldn't expose me during such an embarrassing moment? No student would appreciate- Oh crap.

"Can I help?" Mrs Hinley approached my ex-foster carers.

Dracian walked in behind the pair, his lips pulled into an amused smirk. His eyes sought mine, his smile brightening when our gazes clashed. He was about to turn to the three adults when I shook my head roughly. What would he do? Would he dob me in?

"She was here a moment ago," Mrs Hinley said, searching the hall.

Extending my spell out to her, I channelled my magic. My arms shook at the effort, I was running low. I could always feel when my magic started to evaporate, it felt like I hadn't eaten in days. If I wanted to keep Toby hidden, I had to hide myself.

"I think I saw her go out back." Dracian swept into their conversation, giving them all a charming smile.

Typical of him to use his smarm, but I had to be grateful, it helped distract them. In fact, all three of them fawned over him. What was it with him attracting everyone to him? Couldn't anyone see that he was fake?

155

Instead of standing there, ruminating on his very existence, I had to find somewhere to hide.

Looking around, I spotted an old altar made of stone. It was at the head of the ballroom but was no longer in its proper place. I hadn't known that the academy had been built around a church. It certainly wasn't as sacred as it would've been back in the medieval times. Almost everything had been taken out, even the stained glass windows at the sides. However, a stained glass rose was high above the altar, the sun's rays reflecting coloured light onto the stone floor.

Running over to the altar, I pushed out as much magic as I could, but the students' eyes followed me, their frowns full of confusion.

Once I reached my hiding place, I ducked down behind it and let go of the spell, sighing in relief.

Mrs Hinley called my name once more, asking if anyone had seen me. No one replied, which made a bloody lump come to my throat. Were the students of the Undercover Witch Academy helping me? I would have to swallow all my bitter pills about the students of society after today. Well, maybe for today...

Looking to the left, I stared through the tall window that led to the rose garden. A dark shadow hovered by the glass, drawing close to it and – A chill went up my spine as bright blue eyes appeared in the shadow, watching me closely. Who was it?

"What are we hiding from?" Dracian crawled around the altar, making me jump so hard, I gasped loudly. Glancing around the side, he darted back, his eyebrows wiggling. "Be careful, there's... there's... students out there!"

Trying my hardest not to smile as he pretended that we were under attack, I punched him on the arm. He had no idea that a shadow – which was now gone – had been spying on me. Could it be the snake-napper?

He smiled back, his eyes dancing in amusement. For a split second, his beauty distracted me so much, I forgot where I was as quiet laughter filtered through me.

"If you circle the right, I'll circle the left and we'll herd them all together. That way, those nice people looking for you will be hemmed in with the enemy."

"Enemy?" I shook my head, my breath rushing in and out as he moved closer. The shadow man was completely forgotten now.

Pushing my spine into the altar, I was almost lying down.

He leant over me, bringing his head to hover just above mine. "Everyone's your enemy, right?"

Swallowing really hard, I opened my mouth to reply. Nothing came out. I must have looked like a young girl, not an eighteen year old woman, just coming into her own as she endeavoured to endure life on campus with other witches. Instead, I hid from adults, unable to reply to the hot guy slash killer, who currently held his plump, far too pretty lips right near mine.

"I would ask if the cat's got your tongue," Dracian said, chuckling to himself. "But I know you don't have a familiar."

Fury surged through me, my mouth dropping open wide. I was about to thrust up from where I sat, but Mrs Hinley's voice came closer as she led the parents out of the double doors at the side of the ballroom. Instead, I was stuck staring into Dracian Dread's eyes.

"I didn't mean that the way it came out," he said, raising his hands in surrender as I violently pushed him away from me.

Checking around the other end of the altar, I got up as soon as I saw that the room had been cleared.

Professor Seaton strode in from the entrance hall, just as Dracian came out from behind the altar. Raising his greying eyebrows, he shook his head in dismissal and gestured for us both to go to him.

"As you're here," he said to Dracian. "You can help Alishia get the snake down. Work together to find the clues that might have been left."

Clicking his tongue, he eyed my attire. "Isn't that a little high?"

"It's standard issue," I told him, frowning down at my skirt. Now I really was back in high school.

The cute black boots came to my ankle, hiding the little socks that kept my feet from sweating buckets. It was so old fashioned to have a uniform in higher education, but apparently, if we wanted to represent the academy, we had to wear some sort of uniform. My leather jacket didn't adhere to the rules, but the professor wore one himself, so he wasn't about to berate me.

"Hhhmmm... why did I allow Mrs Hinley to take the lead on such things? Aren't you too old to be wearing a uniform anyway?"

Taking off his blazer, Dracian threw it over his shoulder. He had obviously shoved it on over his jeans and T-shirt in an attempt to look a little like he had conformed.

"Can we retrieve Toby now, please?" I interrupted, not at all impressed that the men were talking about clothes at such an important time.

"Ah, yes." Professor Seaton tapped a drumbeat on his rotund belly. "I've got a ladder just outside, I'll be right back."

He shuffled from the room, his strides slow considering we had to get the snake down as quickly as possible. Mrs Hinley had seemed rather harassed that such a thing had happened in the ballroom.

"Did you hear that two students have lost their magic?" Dracian stared up at the snake, his dark eyes completely focused on the dead familiar. "Do you think it's connected?"

Two? I had told Isabel and Helissa about what I'd overheard between the professors the morning before, but the day had proceeded without a hitch. We had gone to our classes, keeping our ears open and our eyes peeled, but nothing had shown up. How did Dracian Dread know about the witches?

"I... who was the second witch?"

He narrowed his gaze on me. "So, you knew about the first."

Shaking my head, I cleared my throat and put my hands on my hips. "I overheard something about a witch losing their magic, but I don't know how it happened."

My scathing glare did nothing to smooth his cocky grin. He knew more than me, but that was okay, because he was sharing the information. I would use that to my advantage.

"Are you going to tell me about the other witch?"

The scraping of metal on the ground came to us from the hallway. It seemed Professor Seaton was taking his time getting the ladder.

Folding his arms across his chest, Dracian watched me with his dark eyes. "A lad was eating in the cafeteria last night when he collapsed. He had complained about feeling weak all day. When they took him to the infirmary, they could barely trace his magic. He was depleted."

Professor Seaton came into the ballroom, dragging the ladder with him.

Dracian rushed to help him, all smiles. It was almost sickening that the boy had

163

almost charmed me too. I had to keep my guard if I wanted to keep my distance enough to expose him. It had been tricky to investigate him, having been too wrapped up in finding Toby.

That pang of guilt flushed through me, making me shudder as I glanced up at the dead snake. It had been my fault that he was currently hung over the chandelier. I had to come clean to Helissa.

"Alishia," the professor said as Dracian set up the step ladder right next to me. "Make sure to tell Dracian everything you see up there. Once the snake is down, I can go up and do a magic trace to see if our database has a match."

"Database?"

Starting up the ladder, I kept my feet firmly on the steps, not able to look up. As bad as I felt, picking up the dead snake wasn't exactly a thrilling idea. Yes, I wanted to be an agent and learn everything I needed to learn to become successful, but dead animals... eww.

"The academy and most agencies have their own magic database as well as blood and fingerprints. We are able to swab magic and check the imprint through our database. All students would've sent a swab when they applied to the academy." Professor Seaton raised his eyebrows when I glanced down at him.

"Except me, I suppose," I said, pausing on the steps.

Inclining his head, he brushed a hand through his straggly greying hair. "It took us a long time to determine whether you were right for our academy."

Yeah, it really had. They had literally left it to the last minute, which had been kinda cruel, considering I wanted to escape the hellish home of foster care, a place I had come to detest. Who wanted to live with a man who drank heavily and kept the door

165

open while on the toilet? Not me, that's for sure.

"Go on, say it," I said to Dracian, my fingers tightening around the metal rung of the ladder. "They made a mistake in thinking that I was."

Shrugging, Dracian pointed at the snake. "Can we get on with it? I'm missing out on my favourite class."

"Favourite class?" I snorted. "You have witch literature with me, how can that...? You know what," I muttered, returning to my climb. "...never mind."

The floor got further and further away, the stone tiles growing smaller as I reached the high-vaulted chandelier.

Dracian held the ladder firmly for me, especially when it wobbled slightly. Bloody thing, if I fell off and snapped my neck, I hoped my ghost would come back and haunt the pair of them. I wanted my death to be more glamorous. Maybe in a gun fight with a rogue vampire who snapped my neck or something.

"What do you see?" Professor Seaton called when I came in line with the hanging snake.

Considering the school was full of magic people, it went beyond reason that it was me who was perched on top of a crazy tall stepladder, surveying a dead snake. Ah, it was because I was disposable. That had to be it.

Steadying myself, I stared at Toby. "A dead snake."

The professor sighed loudly, rubbing his hand over his beard. "Anything else? Don't look with normal eyes, question everything."

Licking my lips, I concentrated, looking at everything around the snake. "He has a slit across his throat."

"Is there anything on the arm of the chandelier?" Dracian called.

167

Glancing down, I raised my eyebrows at the boy. He held a tablet in his hand, typing something on it as I stared at him. He was such a hypocrite. A part of me believed that it had been him who arranged it, especially as he had run after the snake-napper. The boy we had chased hadn't shown up again, but we had planned to sneak into the secretary's office to check out student files to try and find him. Was he the one who had threatened me with the note?

"There's a smudge of blood, maybe a finger print could be lifted off it. There's nothing else that I can see."

Professor Seaton went over to the corner of the room. Picking up a blanket, he slowly came back over. "Okay," he muttered. "Well done for trying."

Was that a half-arsed attempt at telling me that I'd done a crap job? Yep, it seemed like it.

Dracian frowned up at me, tapping the edge of the ladder. "Let me go up," he said to the professor.

Shaking his head, the professor lifted the blanket towards me, encouraging me to take it. "If there's nothing else, you'd better fetch him down. You don't have magic that will interfere with the imprint. I'll be checking it out. Dracian, you can stay and watch."

Heat exploded through me. How dare he just dismiss me as if I were useless? I had never tried to investigate anything before. I would prove the bastard wrong.

"Give me a moment," I said quietly, going back to inspecting the snake. "Wait, he has a... I wonder if that was there before. He has an A scratched onto his head. That's so crucl. How could someone-?"

"Concentrate." The professor's stern tone snapped me out of my tirade.

Swallowing, I reached towards the chandelier. "Can I touch it?"

"Only if you're extremely careful. You should have gloves on, but we didn't have time to get you any."

Swallowing, I froze when a dark shadow shot past the doors that led to the entrance hallway. Was someone out there, listening in? Maybe it was the snake-napper? Shuddering as the hairs on the back of my neck rose, I couldn't help but feel like someone had been watching me.

"Hello?" Dracian called, snapping me out of my fear-induced stupor.

Returning my attention to the task at hand, I tried to shake off my suspicion. Sliding the snake over, I clenched my teeth when two small words were revealed. Etched into the scaly skin, they glared at me, obviously cast from a spell. *Tell Me.*

The words were tiny, and as I watched, they faded from sight. That meant the message had been for *me*. I had seen spells that disappeared once the receiver had got the message. Great, how did I tell the professor? Could I tell him? Not with Dracian around.

"Toby has been looped over, maybe that means something?"

My heart beat loudly in my ears. I knew what the clue led to. It was the person who wanted to know how I had managed to create magic from sources other than people. How could I tell the professor that when Dracian stood there? I was sure that he had something to do with it.

"We've got that noted down," Dracian said. "Anything else? Are his eyes open or closed? Does the chandelier have any debris on it?"

Trying my hardest not to squirm, I concentrated again. "His eyes are shut, although I don't know why that would make a difference considering he's dead."

The professor chuckled before he spoke. "These are all viable questions that should be asked. Good job, Mr Dread."

171

Oh course, Mr Dread gets the credit. The son of a bitch had well and truly wormed his way into the professor's affections. Not for long, Mr Dracian Dread. As soon as I had proof that it was you that killed my parents, I would tell the whole academy before getting you arrested. It would be a joy to see teacher's pet sent to prison.

"Sir," Dracian said quietly. "I'm concerned about the rumours that are circulating. Apparently, two people have lost their magic in the space of a few days. Do you know what could've caused it?"

My gaze shot down, straight at the professor, who instantly glanced up at me. His cheeks turned pink as he coughed and shook his head. "No, we have no clues yet. Please, let's get on with this."

Why had he looked at me? Were he and Mrs Hinley still suspicious of me? Surely not. I had an alibi... didn't I? I had no idea when the students had actually lost their magic,

172

which didn't look good for me. However, I did know that it wasn't me who had taken their magic, so there was some other explanation for it. I just didn't know what.

"There's nothing else here," I said, agitated by the conversation. "Shall I bring him down?"

Nodding, the professor wiped the sweat from his brow. "Yes, the parents will be filtering back through soon, make haste."

Moving down the ladder, I snatched the blanket from him and went back up to retrieve Toby. It wasn't easy picking up my roommate's dead familiar and placing him in the blanket, but once I did, I cradled it to me, willing him to somehow be alive. If he was truly dead, which he was, worse could happen if I kept ignoring the person trying to find out my secret. I would write them a note, but it would be worded very differently to how they expected it.

"Careful now," the professor said as they both held the ladder. "We don't want any injuries, and we need that snake intact so we can-"

"I know, I know." Taking each step, I tried to ignore the flush of anger that heated my skin. "So you can use proper magic to carry out the investigation."

"Don't underestimate yourself." Taking my arm without flinching, he helped me down. "You were invited here because we think you'd make an exceptional agent if taught the right skills."

Snorting, I held onto Toby as I reached solid ground. "If you say so. He's gone mad, Dracian," I said to my enemy, forgetting myself.

Dracian stayed quiet, watching me as if I was a fascinating television show.

The professor smiled at me, a small sad smile. As if he pitied the life out of me, when really... who was I kidding? Most witches

174

pitied me and my missing magic. It was no wonder I had a chip on my shoulder.

"Can I take him to see Helissa before you start your investigation?"

The professor went to protest but stopped when Dracian piped up. "I think that might be kind, sir. It might help Helissa to say goodbye."

Running a hand over his face, the professor blinked as if he hadn't slept at all. Maybe he hadn't. With a missing familiar and two students who had lost their magic, the academic year hadn't got off to a good start.

"Very well, but don't let anyone else touch him, do you hear me? I won't be able to tell what's happened to him if you do."

Agreeing, I thanked him before rushing from the ballroom.

Footsteps behind me made me look over my shoulder. Dracian followed me, tablet in hand.

175

"What are you doing?" I asked as I sped up, heading towards the stairs in the right wing.

His footsteps were loud as we almost ran, me trying to get away from him, him trying to catch up. His breath came close to my neck as he eventually reached me at the bottom of the stairs.

"What do you want?" Spinning, I faced him, Toby still cradled to me.

"You act so cold, and yet, you hold that snake as if it were a live baby." His dark brooding presence was starting to get on my nerves. My body shook as the grainy image of him crossing in front of my home's CCTV camera made me clench my hands in the blanket.

Frowning, I shrugged, raising my eyebrows. "And...?"

"You've got a real problem with me, even though you don't know me."

"Oh, I know you." My voice was tense, but I quickly cleared my throat, turning back towards the stairs. "Leave me alone, I need to get Toby back to Helissa."

His footsteps still sounded behind me as I ran up the stone steps. He wasn't going to give up that easily. My stupid mouth would get me in trouble before I had the chance to do anything. My revenge had kept me going for years, although, I had read a few self-help books recommended to me by my therapist. I mostly took on board that I had to forgive people. Who the hell was I kidding? I was a witch without magic and a grudge that might get me killed. As if I was going to allow a young boy to get away with murder. Literally.

"I heard about what happened to you."

Snarling, I kept going, refusing to be dragged into a conversation that I didn't want to have. He would play ignorant, pretending to not know who my parents were. If he dared to try and pity me, he would probably get his balls ripped off. Some would say that was harsh, but he deserved it.

"I'm sorry about your parents," he called as I came to the top of the stairs.

Spinning, I glared down at him. All the fury of the past five years bubbled in my chest, making it hard for me to breathe. "Leave me alone, Dracian Dread, you hideous person!"

Okay, so the insult was a little lame, but storming away was satisfying. The past few days had been extremely tough. And to top it off, the teachers suspected it was *me* who was taking the students magic. When would my life get better?

My feet rushed down the hallway, my fist pounding on our door as soon as I reached it. I had to try and channel some of my fury before I went back to class. I also had to calm myself enough to give Toby to Helissa.

"Who is it?" Isabel called.

When I replied, the door opened quickly.

My gaze landed on Helissa, who sat huddled on the bed, her arms wrapped around her knees and a puff of curly brown hair tied in a bun on her head.

"I have him," I whispered, the anger that had filled me moments before flowing straight out of me.

Jumping from the bed, she came over. The blanket hid most of her familiar, but her eyes screwed up as she cried out, reaching forward to stroke him.

I hesitated, debating whether to follow Professor Seaton's request that no one touch the snake. Sod that, his owner had every right to touch him. Although, I would check with her first.

"Helissa, Seaton said that we shouldn't touch him if we want to try and get the best imprint of magic from him."

Raising her eyebrows, she shook her head.

"No? I didn't think so, either, but you know, I had to check."

Handing her the blanket, I backed away. It was a tiny bit odd that she was cradling a snake, but as the tears flowed, my chest squeezed tight.

Isabel took my hand. Heat exploded before I took my hand away. When I was emotional, my touch wasn't safe. It was why no one had touched me properly for years.

"Do you know anything?" Helissa said, turning to me.

They both stared at me, their big brown eyes wide. I couldn't very well not tell them, could I? I would be the shittiest friend in London if I kept it from them.

"I got this note yesterday." Taking it out of my pocket, I handed it to Isabel.

My lip was trapped in my teeth as she read it, her eyes growing even more wider, if that was possible. Here came the explosion, the accusations, the, *it's all your fault...*

Instead, she handed the note to Helissa. Her gaze traced it, her jaw tightening. "Why didn't you tell us about this?"

"I... don't... I can't..."

"She can't trust anyone." Isabel sat on my bed, frowning when she stared at the plain cover. Dismissing it with a wave, she went on. "Ever since her parents died, she's harboured secrets that people would kill her for. She doesn't know how to open up anymore."

My friend was talking like I wasn't in the room, but her words caused a lump to form in my throat. She was right, every last word was annoyingly right. I had become a hard bitch since that night.

"What happened to your parents, Alish?" Isabel tugged me onto my bed, forcing me to sit next to her.

Helissa came over, Toby still in her arms. Seeing the way she grieved her familiar cracked my heart open. I understood so very well what it felt like to cradle something dear to you once they'd gone.

"We had been out for the day to visit my grandma. She was ailing, her health deteriorating, so they dragged me to see her. Of course, being thirteen, I rebelled, plugging music into my ears and ignoring them the whole time." Laughing when they smiled, I sobered quickly as the day played in my mind, like it always had, over and over. "When we got home, we had pizza, but I took mine to my room. My parents had been helping me practice my channelling, my magic was getting stronger."

Swallowing, I sucked in a breath as the memories unfolded. The others watched me speak, their gazes glued to my mouth. "I fell asleep without saying goodnight to them. When I went down in the morning, I... they... ugh, there was blood everywhere in the living room. I followed the trail that had started in the kitchen." Gulping in air, I tried to breathe as my hands started to shake.

Isabel put her hands on my arm, ignoring me when I raised my eyebrows. She wouldn't pull away, it wasn't her style. That was why she had allowed me to borrow her magic when we were children. She was a giving, loving soul, even if she did have a social media addiction.

"My mother was sprawled on the sofa, her eyes... no, I can't."

"We don't need all the details," Helissa said, sitting next to me.

Nodding, I sucked back a sob as tears came to my eyes. "My father was dead nearby, obviously attempting to reach her. His arm stretched out towards the sofa from where he laid on the floor."

The tears dribbled from my eyes and over my cheeks. "Dad had been concerned that we were being watched. He thought it might have been the institute."

"Were there any clues? What did you do?" Helissa sat against the wall, rubbing my back before lifting her hand away.

It was strange having the comfort of people who weren't afraid of me.

For the first time since my parents had died, I allowed myself to cry in front of others. The tears flowed as I forced out the words. "I rang the police. I could see... the blood, it was..." Shaking my head, I tried to clear the image. "... They had been there for several hours, probably dying the night before."

Isabel gasped, her hand coming to her mouth. "Oh, Alishia, I wish you'd told me."

I had kept my distance from my old friend, especially when her parents had been refused permission to adopt me. It had broken my heart to know that the system wasn't going to allow me to be with my second family.

"Before they arrived, I went to my dad's office and checked the CCTV. It was impulsive, but he had always warned me not to completely trust Paranormal MI5. They always work to cover up anything not in alignment with their cause."

"Did you see anything?" Helissa was gripped, leaning forward on the bed as she wiped her eyes.

Scrubbing my face with my hands, I allowed myself to calm. The image of Dracian walking in front of our house at midnight, a rucksack thrown over his shoulder, came into my mind. I wasn't going to divulge that information to the girls, they wouldn't understand why I had waited so long to call him out.

"There was a man. He walked past with a backpack before turning around and coming back ten minutes later. I'm convinced he's the one who came onto our property and killed my parents."

My fingers had curled into fists as I sniffled. I was eighteen years old now, but the fury that laced my veins had lived with me since I had watched that video.

Shuffling forward, Helissa held the blanket tightly against her. "Did they find the man in the video?"

I had already told them too much. Paranormal MI5 had turned up, actually being helpful for a change, and did their thing. They had several clues, but it took them a long while to tell me that they had no idea who the killer was. According to them, whoever killed my parents had been able to cover their tracks.

"No, I did some research myself. I'm still working on it."

Dracian Dread would not be introduced to the conversation. My own search had been arduous. I had managed to copy the CCTV image before MI5 took it. I had found Dracian by pure luck. On a dating app.

Using a fake profile, I had searched the internet for a picture of a dark haired boy with three piercings in his ear. That had been the only clue that had led me to him. Once we had matched, I had managed to find out that he was going to the academy. It had taken me almost five years to find him.

"You're telling me that the officials haven't found your parents' killer?" Helissa snapped.

Moistening my lips, I pushed myself off the bed. "No, they haven't."

Isabel wiped her eyes of the tears that sat in them. Grabbing my hands and forcing me to hold hers, she looked up at me. "You have enemies, but we're your friends. You can trust us."

Blinking back the tears that threatened again, I swallowed as I looked at Helissa. "I'm so sorry your familiar was killed because of me."

Getting up, Helissa put a hand around my waist. "We'll find the bastards who killed

Toby. We'll get the wankers who did such gruesome things to your parents. And, we'll catch the arsehole who dared threaten to blow up the academy."

8

"How are your classes going?" Frankie asked as I poured my last pint of the evening.

It was fairly quiet in the bar, the students all tired from the first week of learning.

Yawning, I shook my head as I handed the beer to a girl who smiled as she handed me her coins.

My boss sat on the other side of the bar, insisting that he had to rest to make sure I was doing a good job. I had learnt a lot tonight. The first and most poignant lesson:

Frankie was a lazy bartender, preferring to let me do all the work.

"Today, we practiced a telekinesis and levitation spell." Throwing the rancid smelling cloth in the air, I attempted to spell it to float.

It fell flat to the ground. It was safe to say, my magic skills were still poor. Although, I had managed to keep a pen floating an inch from the desk for three point five minutes in class. Considering I didn't have much magic left, I had been suitably proud of myself. Not that a levitating pen would be of any help in the predicament I found myself in.

"How do you work at the academy? Surely, you can't do spells unless they allow you to steal magic from someone?"

Oh, yeah, it was probably best I kept my guard up around Frankie. I might be able to fool the students, although, they kinda knew who I was, so it wasn't exactly hard to figure out that I was *that* illusionist witch, but it probably wouldn't stretch to another seasoned illusionist witch.

The students didn't know what I was capable of, but my infamous name had crossed their lips a time or three.

"That's classified," I said, taking a sip from the gin and tonic I had just poured.

Narrowing his gaze on me, Frankie opened his mouth to speak. Before he could, I pointed at the clock and smiled. It was the end of my shift, which meant I could have a gin or ten. Perks of working in a bar? Booze. All. The. Time.

"You're not about to drink my bar into the red."

"You're no fun. Where's your sense of adventure?" Downing the drink, I poured us both another.

Checking the bar, Frankie waved his hand, indicating that I should pass him the drink. His magical doppelganger wasn't in tonight. He was saving his magic for a busier day. Apparently, he had a friend who gave him one hit of magic a week. It sounded a bit like a dodgy drugs deal to me. Surely, witches didn't live that way?

"Frankie?" I started tentatively. "Do you have to pay your friend for... you know?"

As his cheeks burned pink, he looked down at the bar. Nodding without replying, he swallowed hard as sweat lined his forehead. "In this world, we sometimes have to do things that we don't want to do. Trust me, don't do what I do, just accept that you'll never be a happy witch."

Sucking my lip into my mouth, I kept my secret close to my heart. Was it cruel that I wasn't instantly telling him that I had a way for us to live differently? For us to be able to produce magic without taking it from others?

When he dipped his head and stared at the bar, my stomach dropped to my patent leather boots. I didn't know the man well, but I knew exactly what he felt as he leant on the bar, his gaze distant. One day. I had to give my gift to others when I could, but not before I had worked out my own life.

"Life sucks," I said, pouring another drink. "Let's drink."

Shaking his head, Frankie pushed the drink away. "No, alcohol solves nothing. In fact, it's a depressant."

Sucking the drink down, I shrugged. "It might well be, but it does make me feel good for a moment. It's good to let go occasionally."

I didn't need a lecture on drinking, but I understood what Frankie meant. When I was fifteen, I had snuck out of my foster home and drank with teens from my school. We had to answer for plenty of wrongdoings, and I had to keep my head about me when I drank, so maybe Frankie was right.

"I'd better get going," I said, grabbing up my bag. "Thanks for the drink."

Saluting me, he nursed his glass as I left without looking back. The witch was lost in his thoughts as he sipped the gin. He was a man who owned a bar and wasn't an alcoholic. It was pretty unheard of.

Dancing past the last few stragglers, I laughed when they shouted goodbye to me. Yeah, they didn't know me, but it was nice to hear a friendly goodbye. Especially as my boss was having a moment.

Pushing my way out into the open air, I breathed in deep. My first pay packet would arrive in just two days, which meant I could invest in a new bag. The one currently sitting on my shoulder was barely hanging on to its strap.

Not only that, I could get myself a spell book. For the first time in my life, I would actually find a way to learn magic properly. I'd had enough of the students frowning at me, and it had only been three days since I'd started the academy.

The cool breeze brushed my skin as I put on my jacket, ready to return to the dorm and sleep. The day had been filled with classes, so we'd all been too busy to discuss our private investigation of the snake-killer. Yeah, the bastard had a new name.

My phone had multiple texts from them, urging me to meet them for breakfast first thing in the morning.

"Those girls can't live without me," I muttered, smiling to myself briefly.

Helissa had given Toby to Seaton, making him swear that he told her everything. Of course, the head of the school agreed, but my suspicions were raised. Rumours had started to circulate about the two students who had lost their magic. Eyes had turned to me occasionally throughout the day. Surely, the students didn't suspect me too?

My phone suddenly burst into noise, making me jump as I neared the academy gates. Answering it, I sang a greeting.

A footstep made me turn, my heart suddenly flipping in my chest when a young couple walked past, hand in hand, giggling to themselves. Oh crap, I had just made a total idiot of myself. Well done, Alishia. My reputation was going to be crushed now they'd heard me sing... terribly, I might add.

"Alishia?" Isabel called down the phone. "Are you back yet?"

"Nope," I replied, smiling awkwardly when the couple glanced over their shoulders.

They headed towards the side entrance to the dorm wing, their laughter filtering back to slide in my ear and make me want to crawl underground. Instead, I followed at a very slow pace, not wishing to disturb their piss-taking... of me.

"I just embarrassed myself by apparently auditioning for the X Factor, true Alishia style."

"I thought you sounded quite good," Isabel replied. "You'll be knocked out in the first round, but it's all about the taking part."

Chuckling, I glanced up at the building. The dark shadows of the walkway were lit by solar lights in the ground, but it was eerily quiet as the couple disappeared from sight.

"Well, I'll have you know, I'm-" My sentence stopped as I searched for my dorm room window.

It was only two flights up, but underneath, on the ground below, stood a silhouetted figure, a hood over his head as it tilted back to look up. Was he looking at my window? The light was on inside, Helissa obviously not in bed yet.

"Are you okay? You've gone all quiet on me." Isabel's tone changed, growing concerned.

It had been such a strange start to the year, everyone was on edge. My whole body tingled from adrenaline as I sucked the

197

electric from my phone, forcing the battery to die. Tucking the phone away, I swallowed hard.

The boy, I was assuming it was a boy because he was fairly tall, shuffled his feet. When he glanced over his shoulder, I ducked behind a small bush. I hadn't had time to see his face, so I didn't know who it was. Chancing it, I snuck a glance around the foliage. He had gone back to looking up at the dorm window.

What made him think that he had the right to stalk us? I could see him clearly as he bent down and took something out of what looked like a backpack.

No, I wouldn't allow him to hurt us. Helissa was already suffering from the loss of Toby. Her parents hadn't even bothered to come and see her, preferring to snub their daughter. Apparently, she wasn't living up to the Wayward name.

Stepping out from my hiding place, I made a run for the boy as he lifted something that was pointy towards the window. I didn't have much magic, but I wouldn't waste it.

My footsteps sounded on the earth, alerting him to my presence.

Spinning, he aimed the pointy thing at me.

Ignoring the thud of my petrified heart, I kept going. My hand shot out as I whispered the telekinesis spell I'd learnt earlier in the day. A bright spark started to form at the end of his stick. Ah, the boy had a wand. Well, not for long. The wand clattered to the floor as my spell took all of my magic, forcing it from his hand.

"What-?" His sentence was cut off as I tackled him to the ground, my arms wrapping around his legs.

He grunted as we crashed on the grass, his back smashing onto the earth and breaking our fall. I tried gripping his wrists, but my fingertips heated as his magic slunk into me. Shit, if I pinned him down, I would ultimately take his magic at the same time. Did he deserve my worry in this matter? Would an agent ask nicely? No! He had been about to cast a spell on our dorm, he must have been the culprit who took Toby.

"If you don't tell me who you are, I'm going to take your magic," I said, pressing my fingers into his wrists. "All of it!"

He instantly stopped bucking to get me off. It would've only taken a moment to dislodge me, being that I was puny compared to him, but the heat of my hands forced him to stop. I would use his magic against him if he didn't answer my questions.

"Okay, stop!" Going still, he opened his hands in a show of submission.

Releasing one of his wrists, I stayed sitting on his chest. It wasn't the most ladylike of positions, but if I wanted to be a good agent, I had to learn how to interrogate bad people on the job.

"Who are you?" I spat, leaning closer.

He tried to wrench his wrist out of my hand, but I held tight. I softened my energy, trying not to take too much of his magic. The rumours about me stealing would circulate even more if the rat squealed. However, he was the one who needed to give me answers, I was just using my skills in the fight for freedom or whatever.

"My name's James. James Hinley-Seaton."

Ugh, the professor's son? Wait, he had both surnames. Was he the spawn of both our teachers? That made things a little more complicated considering I was sitting on him and stealing his magic. Poo.

Although, wait. Looking closer, I frowned. He was the same James who had comforted Helissa when Toby had been taken. What was he doing outside our dorm?

"Are you the snake-napper? Tell me the truth!"

Shaking his head, he frowned at me. "No, you've met me before, I'm a friend of Dracian's. He paid me to spy on you."

"He did?"

Wincing, he looked at where I clenched his wrist in my hand.

Releasing him, I jumped off, expecting him to either attack me or run away. I wouldn't blame him, I had acted like a crazy bitch. Although, I couldn't help but be a little proud that I'd brought him down.

"I knew he was the one to take Toby. He made you do it, didn't he?"

Sitting up, the boy frowned as he brushed grass off the legs of his black jeans. "We've got nothing to do with your friend's familiar."

Hhmm... Did I trust his word? Why else would Dracian want James to spy on me?

There was one way to check if he was lying to me. A truth spell. It was the one spell that my parents drummed into me. They had often cast it on me, to make sure that I told them how I was coping with their training. They wanted to make sure I wasn't trying to please them. They never asked me anything else when I was under the spell, but they had to protect me. Being shunned by the coven had driven them to do anything to keep me safe. My chest squeezed as I remembered the way they hugged me before bed, the family bear hug they'd called it.

"Are you okay?"

Ah, yeah, I had a criminal right next to me. Maybe I should pay attention to the present moment, instead of slipping back to the past.

Reaching for his arm, I whispered the truth spell, using his own magic to create it.

He frowned when I let go, his head shaking as he got to his feet. "What are you doing?"

"Are you responsible for snake-napping Toby?" Pushing up from the ground, I faced him, my hands on my hips.

He looked down at me, his eyes studying my face, his expression clearly showing how crazy he thought I was. Hey, I wasn't the one standing under someone else's dorm window late at night. He could talk.

"No, Dracian wanted me to make sure you were okay. He's fascinated by you and-" Clamping his hand over his mouth, he glared at me. "You put a truth spell on me!"

Shrugging, I flicked my hair behind my shoulder. Yep, if anyone messed with me, I would... put a truth spell on them? My agent training was limited, but I was enjoying the practice.

"So, you're not involved with the snake or anything else?"

My questioning technique lacked a little, but with the truth spell, he would still be able to give me clues. Especially about the boy who had killed my parents. In fact, it was almost tempting to try and learn everything about him.

Tugging his hoody off his head, James revealed his bright blonde hair. "How many times do I have to say it? I'm literally spying on you because Dracian paid me."

"Do you know much about Dracian?"

Clamping down his jaw, James went to turn away. Grabbing his hood, I pulled it, which did absolutely nothing considering he was a fair few feet taller than me. Scoffing, he looked over his shoulder, shaking his head.

"Woman! What are you doing? I don't see why I have to answer your questions." He screwed up his face before blurting the answer to my question. His will power hadn't lasted long. "Dracian is a cool guy, he really wanted everyone to get to know each other before the school year started."

"I bet he did," I muttered. "Has he ever told you about his past? When he was about thirteen?"

Backtracking, James held up his hands. "No. Now, I'm going."

"No!" Throwing a freezing spell on him, I smiled to myself when he went still.

Wow, maybe I wasn't as bad at magic as I'd thought. My phone battery had given me more magic than usual. Not that I'd often used magic on other people, preferring to practice on inanimate objects to keep everyone safe. Ever since I realised that I could take life force from animals, I hadn't touched one. Ever.

"Call Dracian," I ordered him. "Tell him to meet us in the rose garden, by the fountain."

"Fine." Muttering under his breath, he took out his phone. "Anything to shut you up."

Fighting the urge to smile, I kept my stance strong, my hands still on my hips. Yeah, I could be an agent. It was easy!

As the phone rang, he avoided looking at me. I kept staring at him, trying to intimidate him. Wasn't that what I was supposed to do?

"Mate, I've got Alishia here, she's demanding that you meet us in the rose garden." He grunted. "Yeah, by the fountain." Clearing his throat, he grunted again. "Yeah, well, she caught me!"

His agitation was actually quite funny, but when he hung up, he glared at me. "Don't laugh. He said he's coming down now."

Tempted to order him to follow me to the rose garden, I stopped myself just in time. My mother had taught me that the feminine power of receiving and allowing was just as powerful as the masculine power of force.

"Great," I said in a sing song voice. "Thanks!"

Grabbing up my bag, I spun away from him and headed around the side of the dorm wing. The front doors to the academy were locked at eleven every night, which was why

207

I had been heading to the side entrance in the first place.

His thudding footsteps sounded behind me. Ah, my tactic had worked. Well, either that or he was going back to his dorm. Slipping a glance over my shoulder as I passed the entrance to the other end of the dorm wing, I smiled to myself when I saw him dragging himself along behind me.

Game. Set. And, hopefully, match.

My feet sped up as the shadows fell down on us. The side of the building stretched back quite far, the rose garden through an iron gate at the end. A chill made me shudder as I turned to look at the boy again. "How long have you known Dracian?" I asked conversationally.

"About a year. His parents are friends with mine, well, his mum is since his dad, you know..."

Frowning as we approached the gate, I looked at him. "No, I don't know?"

"Really?" His voice was stunned in the dark. "Everyone knows that his dad is in prison."

Coughing, I yanked open the gate. "Oh, right, well, apparently not *everyone* knows all about the famous Dracian Dread."

"I detect a little bit of resentment, Magic Fingers."

"Woah," I said, swinging towards Mr Hinley-Seaton. "That name is not acceptable."

Waving me away, he marched through the gate and skipped down the stone steps into the rose garden.

The darkness enveloped the nooks and crannies. Rows of beautiful bushes led the way to the centre of the courtyard. A huge rose, carved from stone, showered water from the edge of its leaf, straight into the pool below. The insignia of the academy blasted from every part of the garden. Hundreds of different coloured roses twinkled in the moonlight as the clouds uncovered it. Some of the area was paved in cobblestones, some in grass. It was incredible to think that the roses were kept alive, all year round, by magic.

Almost running to the centre, James plonked himself down on the stone edge of the pool.

Joining him, I huffed, folding my arms across my chest as we waited. I had vowed to start carrying my magic-inducer – yes, that was the extremely uncreative name I had come up for it, although it often changed – with me as soon as I'd seen James under my dorm window. It was getting too dangerous to be out and about without some form of instant magic.

"You called?" A deep voice made me jump.

Dracian appeared in front of me, clicking his fingers towards his friend.

I glared at him as James got to his feet and ran off, only glancing back once. Did the teachers' son know what Dracian really was?

My blood thickened in my veins, making the hair on the back of my arms stand up. My leather jacket wasn't good enough to keep me warm in such cold company.

"What do you want? I was about to go to sleep."

Stepping towards the fountain, Dracian flicked a finger and the water started to cascade heavier. The rushing sound covered our words, a tactic that was smart, but put me on edge. If he didn't want anyone to hear us, what was he going to say? Or, even worse, do?

"Why did you pay James to spy on me?"

He glanced over his shoulder from where he stood, his deep dark eyes narrowing on me. A slight lift of his lip made it look like he'd smirked, but it was hard to tell in such poor light. My insides quivered as realisation dawned.

I was standing, alone, in the dead of the night, in the middle of a secluded rose garden, with the killer of my parents. Shit, what had I let myself in for?

A part of me had humanised Dracian, especially after seeing the way he was with everyone else. Friendly, kind, annoyingly handsome with a ton of boyish charm. Ugh, it was stomach rolling.

Coming closer, he leant down and gripped my upper arm. His head lowered before I could pull free, his lips almost brushing my ear. "I'm intrigued by you, Magic Fingers."

"Don't call me that," I bit between my teeth. "I don't like it. I have no magic, remember?"

Releasing me gently, he stepped away, going back to the fountain. Looking up at it, he stared, almost mesmerised by the flow of water as it left the stone leaf.

"You have an ability that not many witches possess. You also created a way for you to hone that, which no other witch has done. It's no wonder the academies wanted you. And the institute."

"What do you know about the institute?" I snapped against my better judgement.

Alishia, time to be cool. I had to play innocent, as if I didn't know a thing. And yet, his silent gazing made me slip closer to him. It was just in case he spoke and I couldn't hear him. Or, that's what I told myself, anyway.

"I know that the institute arrested my father for something he didn't do. They go after any witch who doesn't conform to their ideals. The human government set up the institute to make sure our secret doesn't get out." Crossing his arms over his chest, he kept staring at the rose.

I tried to take my gaze away from his muscly arms, but it was pretty hard. What type of sick person found it hard not to enjoy the sight of the boy who had killed their parents? Oh yeah, me. Bloody female hormones.

Clearing my throat, I tried my best to keep my voice calm. "Why did they arrest your father?"

May as well find out the juicy gossip while I was there. Maybe Dracian would lead himself into a trap of his own making. He might not have even known that I was related to the people he killed.

"They claim that he was helping a few friends of his to make a magic bomb using electric."

My ears pricked up. "Electric?"

Nodding, Dracian turned to me. "Yes, he's classed as a terrorist against humans, even though he didn't do anything."

Almost coughing, I stepped closer. "What was he doing with the electricity?"

"He was helping a friend with an experiment. Apparently, his daughter needed it for something. I didn't ever really understand it, but they were working on creating something. You know what...?" he said, shaking his head. "I'm not going to lie, I tuned him out every time he tried to explain it to me."

My whole body trembled as I tried to keep my breath even. Surely, his father couldn't have been the man who helped *my* father? I vaguely remembered my dad meeting up with a scientist who knew how to safely increase voltage of electricity before it fried someone's brain. He had taught my dad, probably without knowing, how to help me build my tolerance to electric. It had to be my family he was helping, surely?

"When he was arrested, I went off the rails. I was only thirteen, but you know what it's like at that age."

Yeah, and we were a ton more mature now, weren't we? Although, if he had gone off the rails, maybe he knew that it was my dad his father was helping, which made him go to extreme lengths to take out his frustration. It gave him the perfect motivation.

"I knew it," I whispered to myself.

"Knew what?"

Shaking my head, I backtracked. "Nothing."

"What's your problem with me?" he snapped, the nice guy act apparently coming to an end.

Raising my hands, I showed him my palms in mock surrender. If he dared to pull a blood vessel popping spell on me, like he did my parents, I... well, I'd be pretty buggered.

"You..." I tried to search for the right words. "... My father was..."

Did I tell him? Surely, I would be playing my hand too early. If I let him know that I had seen him approach my house, not only that... I'd cast a spell that was strictly forbidden by an illusionist witch... well, he would shop me in to the institute.

My breath rushed out of my lungs as he watched me. I hadn't dared to even remember the memory spell I had cast on my mother. I hadn't meant to do it, but when I wrapped my arms around her dead body, her residue magic slipped into me. I begged to know what had happened, which inadvertently cast the memory spell.

As the image of her pain played in my mind, I clenched my hands into fists.

Dracian's eyebrows lowered as he watched me, concern etched into the frown lines on his forehead.

She had called for my dad when the pain blasted into her head. A bang on the window made her swing to look at the very boy who now stood in front of me. My father's call brought my mother's attention to the doorway. He was on the ground, crawling as he clutched his skull with one hand.

Pain overtook my mother, and the last thing I saw before it went black, was my father's contorted face, blood running from his eyes as he reached out for her, my mother, the woman he loved.

"Alishia." Dracian reached for me. "What's wrong?"

"You!" I hissed through the tears that were forming in my eyes. "You kil-"

"What's going on here?"

Professor Seaton appeared, his dressing gown hanging awkwardly around him. He had attempted to tie it around his rotund stomach, but it was barely closed. He even wore ACDC T-shirts to bed apparently.

"Nothing," I snapped, glaring at Dracian.

His face had been clear as day in the memory. And, after watching the CCTV, I knew that it was him who had cast the spell to kill my parents. He had even just admitted that he went off the rails after his father was sent to prison for helping mine.

Dracian watched me, his facial expression blank. Did he know what I was going to say? Had my emotions got the better of me before I had proper proof?

"Mr Dread, why don't you go back to your dorm? Alishia, come with me."

See? He was the perfect student with a squeaky clean reputation. Considering he had gone off the rails, he must have done a lot to redeem himself. Or maybe Professor Seaton didn't know.

"Sir, I'd like to escort Alishia back to her-"

"I told you to go back to your dorm," the professor ordered.

Inclining his head, Dracian glanced at me before marching away. His quick glance may have looked innocent to Seaton, but I could read the message in his eyes. It wasn't over.

Taking a cigarette packet out of his pocket, the professor lit one. "Did you know..." he started, pointing at the rose fountain as he blew out the smoke. "... that every academy in London had to find a way past the institute to invite you to this year?"

"They did?" I blurted, forcing my hands to unclench as I glanced at the fountain.

I had no idea why the eccentric rocker had pointed at the rose, but apparently, he had something to say.

Nodding, he sucked his bottom lip into his mouth. "We've all heard of your gift. No illusionist witch has ever been able to find a way around their disability."

Almost choking, I glared at him. "Disability? I'm not sure that's the right term, sir."

Waving his hand, he watched as white smoke billowed from the end of his cigarette. "A bit harsh maybe. I can't really think of anything else to call it."

"Maybe nothing? Just because I don't have my own magic, doesn't make me any less of a witch."

"No, no, you're right. I wouldn't have tried so hard to get you into my academy if I didn't know your power." Flicking the ash from the end of his fag, he faced me head on. "Rumours have been abounding, but no one knows your true power. I heard that you did a demonstration, twice, with just the electrical power from your phone."

Ah, his true motives were coming out now. Who would've guessed that the principal of the academy only wanted me for my *unique* talent?

"Why did all the academies want me? What could I possibly do for them?" Of course, I knew the answer. Everyone wanted me for my secret, not because I was Alishia Jones, awesome girl with incredible wit. Or some may say.

"I don't know about them, but I would like to train you to become an agent witch unlike any other. Plus, I knew your father, I feel like I would be letting him down if I didn't protect you from the institute."

Swallowing, I tried to fight the lump that came to my throat. If I got upset every time someone mentioned my parents, I'd be crying all over the place, leaving me open to the bullies of the world.

"Did you know that my foster parents made a deal with them?"

He glanced at the ground, his shaggy grey hair falling forward. "It doesn't surprise me, the institute would've offered them a lot of money."

"Why?" I breathed, staring at him in an attempt to gauge his reaction to my question.

Looking me square in the eye, he blinked once. "To experiment on you. If they had managed to get you, they would've made a weapon out of you. I promise not to do that. When I say that I want you to be the best illusionist agent, I don't want it for myself, I want it for *you*. The underworld is a dangerous place for people like us."

"Us?" As if the professor was an underdog, he was the head of a reputable academy.

Lifting his gaze to look at the rose again, he puffed out the smoke he had just inhaled. "Yes, Alishia," he muttered, meeting my gaze. "You might think that you're alone, but I lost my magic for a time. You... you helped me to get it back."

9

Walking down the corridor, I tried to still my shaking hands. The letter was clenched in my hand, almost crunched up with the force. It had been a fitful night when I had finally managed to sleep.

The professor had told me that my father had helped him to learn how to re-connect to his magic source after an illusionist witch drained him. Without me, my father would never have known how to aid him. Apparently, he was grateful.

"Alishia," Helissa called from behind.

Reaching the Infinity letterbox, which was a traditional red box in the wall, I pushed the note through the hole before my roommate caught up to me. I had decided to reach out to the snake-killer. My nerves had been on edge ever since Toby had been found hanging from the chandelier. If the boy who had taken him could carry out his murderous threat, he would probably blow up the school. I had kindly asked him to meet me so I could tell him my secret. As if I would. Hopefully he would be stupid enough to fall for my trick.

"Why did you leave so abruptly?" Helissa joined me, her hair wild and her eyes searching for something in her bag. "I made this for you."

Handing me what looked like a weird belt, she grinned. I tried not to frown, but the leather contraption looked a little *fifty shades of grey* to me. I wasn't sure I was interested in that sort of thing. Wait, I was totally sure that I wasn't interested.

"I'm sorry, I don't really- er..."

Helissa's eyes widened when she saw how uneasy I was. "Wait." She gasped. "You don't... Dudette, it's a holster for your exterminator thing."

Laughter started in the pit of my stomach and rumbled up my chest, bursting from my mouth as Helissa bit her bottom lip.

"Did you think I was some sort of pervert?"

Nodding, I clenched my stomach as I bellowed with laughter, unable to control myself.

The students in the corridor looked at me, smiles coming to their faces as they absorbed my hilarity. It was contagious, and the more they stared, the more I laughed.

Helissa was giggling now, her hand covering her mouth. Every time our gaze met, we both cracked up even more. It was nice to feel free enough to laugh.

Calling all students, the intercom blared out, jarring us out of our stupor. *Please make your way to the ballroom for an emergency assembly.*

Everyone started to whisper as they turned from the classrooms and headed back towards the entrance hall. I tucked the holster away, thanking Helissa.

I had shown her my magic inducer – I really had to find a better name for it – so she knew what it was I used to create my magic. After explaining that I was being spied on, she had insisted that I carry it with me at all times. The gift she had conjured was incredibly useful.

"I'm just going to go and put this on," I said, ducking into the ladies as I waved.

Going on without me, Helissa tried to blend in with the crowd. Most of the students knew who she was, their glances covert as they admired her from afar. Her witch bloodline was one of the oldest in England.

When inside the toilet, I took off my jacket and clipped the leather holster across my maroon T-shirt. It was a tight top, so the holster sat nicely across my chest. Retrieving my magic blaster from my bag, I tucked it into the pocket that hung on the side, sitting snug against my ribs. It was comfortable and fit perfectly.

A smile came to my face as I came out of the loos and trotted to the entrance hall. Students were inside the ballroom now, their backs to me as I slipped inside. They all sat on chairs, facing the old unused altar. Professor Seaton stood in front of it, already talking loudly.

"Ah, Alishia, please come and sit up here."

Indicating a seat a few rows from the front, he waved his hand impatiently. The whole of the school, all five years, were crammed into the hall. Why would he pick on me?

Heat rushed over my skin as all eyes watched me waltz down the aisle. Oh gosh, why had I worn my skirt stupidly short today? The rebel in me had wanted to provoke Mrs Hinley, who was constantly on our backs about it, but now, I regretted every rebellious part of myself.

Dracian caught my eye, winking when I glared. He was right, our conversation wasn't over. I had twisted and turned in an effort to get him and his dark, dark eyes out of my mind the night before. His revelation that his father had been put into prison for helping someone else, namely my father, sat uncomfortably on my, two sizes too small, chest.

"We have some bad news," the professor went on as I disrupted the whole row of students who had to stand to allow me to sit.

"Seven of our students have lost their magic."

An audible gasp ran around the hall, ranging from small squeaks to bellows of disbelief. Manoeuvring myself around so I faced the hall, ready to sit, I froze when several pairs of eyes narrowed on me. Wait, why were they glaring at me as if I was a stinky sock? Surely-?

"Please." Professor Seaton waved his hands to quieten the mumbling that erupted. "Calm down. We don't know what is causing the problem..." At this, he glanced at me, almost pointedly. "... but we have an investigation under way. If you know anything, please come forward and speak to either Mrs Hinley or myself."

Did he seriously just stare at me as if I was the culprit? Oh great, more and more students had turned to glance at me, their noses in the air as I stared back, widening my eyes for effect.

I was a little tempted to call out the professor, who apparently had a child with Mrs Hinley, but what would I say? Yeah, well you kissed another teacher. Pffft. It was useless, they were going to blame me whatever I said.

What made me squirm the most was how the professor hadn't said anything the night before. Not one little clue that he suspected me of stealing seven students' magic. I mean, what did he think I was doing with that amount of magic? I could create myself a nice little Ferrari or maybe even a unicorn. Oh, now that was an idea.

"We won't be suspending classes just yet, but if it happens again, we'll have to stop them until our investigation is finalised."

"Ironic, isn't it?" one the students at the front shouted. "We've come to an academy to train as agents and we have our first case in these very walls!"

Rumbles of chuckling filtered through the room as the professor waved his arm. "Yes, yes, it's all very funny. Keep your guard up, don't talk to anyone outside the academy if you can help it and for goodness sake, wear protection."

Our jaws dropped as Mrs Hinley, who had been standing nearby, stormed in front of the professor. "What Professor Seaton means is that you shouldn't be doing any of that while this is going on. Who knows how this is happening!"

Students got up to leave as she dismissed us, her pretty face screwing up in disgust as she turned to the professor. They whispered between themselves, their expressions full of angst.

Ugh, if the professor hadn't just started a witch hunt on me, I would've been tempted to help them, but no... I would walk out of the ballroom gracefully and-

"Professor?" Isabel called, thrusting through the leaving students. "Is the ball still going ahead tomorrow night?"

Tempted to illusion myself out of there, I looked around to find Helissa. Several students watched me as they passed, their glares burning through my leather jacket and writing Traitor on my back. Seriously?

"The ball will go ahead!" Mrs Hinley shouted at the top of her shrill voice. "Too much money has gone into the welcome ball," she hissed at Seaton when he went to protest.

Well, as long as the ball was going ahead, all would be well in the world of witchcraft. Oh crap, my pretend joyousness was short lived. That meant Isabel would force me to go to the dance. Americans had invented the heinous evening entertainment to terrorise students, I was sure of it. Like a slow torture method used to make sure their adolescent years kept them downtrodden. I, for one, only wanted to endure the ball to see the boys in their handsome suits. There was just something very Christian Grey about a man in a suit.

"Did you hear that?" Isabel shouted in my direction. "We can still go!"

Ducking my head and pretending I didn't know the apparently thirteen year old pubescent girl, I slunk between two other witches and headed towards the doors.

A tug on my hair caused me to turn, my head almost butting into Dracian's chin. The shock of his annoyingly handsome face made me lose my footing. Oh no, I was going down.

As my legs gave way, I ended up kneeling on the floor.

Dracian was still walking with the flow, his waist at my head height. Err, this was totally uncomfortable and... yep, he literally just walked into my face with his nether regions. So wrong, on so many levels.

His hand wrapped around my arm, grabbing me to my feet. I was traumatised, my eyes completely squeezed shut. I was blinded, not even sure what part of my face had touched... down there.

"I'm keen to know you more," Dracian said, the corner of his lip sinking into his cheek. "But, that was a little forward."

Blinking my eyes open, I allowed him to march me to the entrance hallway where the students thinned out, already going back to their classes. "I think you just blinded me with your bulge."

His cheeks turned a dark shade of pink as Isabel and Helissa joined us. It was good to see the cool boy humbled, and embarrassed, about my misfortune. Maybe he wasn't as cocky- nope, wrong word to use.

"Did you see the way they stared at you?" Helissa said, linking her arm through mine.

Dracian's gaze slid down to see where our arms touched. I watched him as his eyebrows rose slightly before his expression straightened out again. He was probably shocked that someone dared to touch me.

"It's okay," I said, turning my back to Dracian and pulling Helissa towards the learning wing. "It's not possible that it was me, so anyone with any sense would know that."

"I'm not sure there's many people with sense in this building," Isabel said, waving goodbye to Dracian who got waylaid by James Hinley-Seaton.

Marching as a threesome, I kept my head held high as the other students stared. My confidence waned as we neared the classroom. Maybe I *was* the top suspect in the disappearing magic case.

"Have you heard any more from the killer?" Isabel put her phone out in front of us and snapped a selfie.

Great, she would post the picture of me with my mouth wide open and everyone would like it because she's smiling beautifully. Bloody society. Values and morals were completely gone, especially when it came to bigging up our sisters in a positive way.

"I can't believe you just posted that without asking us," Helissa said, shaking her head.

We were about to enter the classroom when I pulled them back to update them. "I've sent the letter to the snake-killer. Hopefully, I'll hear back before anything drastic happens. I've been wondering whether to tell Seaton about the threat."

Both girls insisted that I didn't. Apparently, I was embroiled in every problem that was currently haunting the academy. How had that happened in the matter of days?

"You're right," I whispered as Mrs Hinley called us into the classroom.

We rushed to our seats, our heads ducked as the students watched us, or more specially me. Oh boy, I was in academy trouble. No girl wanted all the attention for all the wrong reasons.

My heart sped up when an official looking tiny woman with dark hair and a leather jacket just like mine, walked in the room. The boys' grumbled appreciation as Mrs Hinley asked the woman to introduce herself.

"My name is Devon Jinx. I'm an agent with the Hunted Witch Agency. I was bloody terrible at anything until I found my job, so don't panic about today, okay?"

Mrs Hinley's cheeks turned pink as she cleared her throat. "Devon is going to tell us a bit about being an agent before you all give us a demonstration of your abilities."

My stomach sank down to my feet as Devon took out a silver dagger. She flicked it in the air and caught it by the handle again, making the whole class gasp. The woman was kick-ass!

"We hunt down rogue witches who are a danger to humans and the underworld." Walking up the aisle between the tables, Devon looked at each one of us. "I've fought various paranormal creatures, seen dead bodies and got myself into a shit-ton of trouble."

"Did you ever kill anyone?" Dracian asked in a deep drawl.

She turned to him, her small frame shifting to stand beside him. Nodding slowly, she glanced around, her eyes landing on me. "Yes, I've killed to protect myself and others. I've made mistakes, I've lost control of my magic. But, mostly, it's been for the greater good."

A chuckle came from Dracian as the class stayed silent, staring at the goddess in front of us. Okay, that was a little OTT but still, she was amazing, and I wanted to be like her.

"Something to add?" Devon asked Dracian.

Pushing to his feet, he towered over the small agent, his dark eyes looking down at her. "No, I just find it hard to believe that someone of your size has such a big... ego."

Ouch, why was the witch being so spiteful?

The students in the room glanced at one another, shocked to see a darker side to Mr Dread. I wasn't though, not when I knew what he had done to my parents.

I couldn't see Devon's face well, but I gasped when she thrust her arm towards Dracian's stomach. He went to defend himself, his hands reaching for her arm. In a split second, she spun around him, jumped on his back – knocking over a chair in the meantime – and hung there with her dagger pushed against his throat.

"Challenge accepted," she said loudly before leaning in and whispering something in his ear before shouting. "Point taken?"

A grin crossed my lips. Dracian's eyes were wide, his chest huffing in and out. Yes, it was good to see the cool and collected student rattled. It served him right for challenging someone he didn't know. Although, if Mrs Hinley hyperventilated for much longer, she would pass out.

"Point taken," Dracian said as Devon dropped off his back.

"You see..." She came closer to our table, looking me in the eye. "When we feel like we're powerless, we've lost. You have to grab the power from within you and force it out into the open for all to see."

Smiling at me, she turned and went to the front of the classroom. Mrs Hinley gripped her wrist, squeezing tightly as she steadied herself. "My goodness, a real display there of what a proper agent looks like."

"When do we learn how to do that?" Isabel called out.

Shaking her head, Mrs Hinley wiped the sweat from her brow with her perfectly manicured hand. "If you make it to Second Year, you start combat training."

"If we make it?" I blurted.

The class turned to look at me.

Okay, so I was *that* student who was stupid. I obviously didn't know how the academy worked, or hadn't taken it in, one or the other. Typical Alishia.

Licking her lips, Mrs Hinley scowled in my direction. "As most of you know, you have to pass First Year in order to progress into Second Year and so on. You are tested throughout the year to gauge your skills. If you're found failing, you have to leave when we tell you to."

Ah crap, I had better come up with a backup plan if I failed to impress. I wasn't

242

exactly good at spells, so that meant I had to work extremely hard to prove myself.

"I'm here to help you with your first test," Devon announced, pointing at me. "Show me what you've got."

Stuttering, I looked at my friends. "I... I'm an illusionist witch, I can't..."

"Sure you can, I've heard the rumours, and we all know rumours are the creation of bored and insignificant people." She glared at Dracian for some strange reason. "Time to put those rumours to bed and show us how incredible you are."

Getting to my feet, I slowly came around the table. When I was behind Isabel, I slipped my hand under my jacket and pressed the button on my Magic Tranquiliser, bracing myself for the electrical current that zipped into my thumb.

The shock made me jerk as I paused, the electricity filtering into my body. I wasn't ready to let people know how I got my magic.

Hopefully, they wouldn't question it today. Not on the day where witches were being drained of their magic.

"Be quick about it," Mrs Hinley barked, snapping her fingers.

A flash of magic sparked from her hand as my feet started to move of their own accord, almost running to the front of the class. I stared at our teacher, my mouth dropped open at her gall. How dare she control me? I would-

"I apologise," she said quickly, laughing awkwardly.

Devon moved in front of the teacher, her dagger still grasped in her hand. "I'm an Essex witch, which means my weapon is a birth right passed down by my family. This dagger has the spell of our family engraved on it. What's your weapon? Other than your awesome jacket, of course."

Someone coughed before saying under their hand, "Other people's magic."

Staring in the direction of the voice, I smiled sweetly. "If you're not careful-"

"That's enough," Mrs Hinley interjected. "Please remember that Alishia has every right to be here."

"It's okay." I told the teacher as I whispered a creation spell.

Rats suddenly appeared all over the floor, running over the students' feet, squeaking madly. Everyone lifted their feet, one girl screaming when a rat ran up her bare leg. Oops, maybe the rats had been overkill. Although, I was enjoying it a little too much.

Blinking, I almost laughed when the rats disappeared. They were gone as quickly as they'd appeared, leaving the students still gasping in fright. The only person who hadn't been afraid was Dracian bloody Dread.

"Nice," Devon said, high fiving me. "Was that real or an illusion?"

Swallowing, I clasped my hands in front of me. "It was an illusion. Most witches can create physical matter, but I find that hard. However, I can form imagery well. If you girls..." I said to three giggling students as they rolled their eyes at one another. "... want to look better, just ask. I'll give you a makeover in the click of a finger."

Isabel's jaw dropped at the same time as the class chuckled.

Biting my lip, I went to move away from the kickass agent, who grabbed me back. I jumped away, jerking my arm from her grip.

"Don't worry," she said to me quietly as Mrs Hinley called for order. "I'm not afraid of anything. Well, that's not technically true. My partner, Mr Gerald Smelly-arse, he's lethal. Not just in the field, but when he lets one go... well, it could literally cause an explosion if he was near an open flame."

The seriousness of her expression made me laugh as I relaxed. The agent was super cool, just like I wanted to be. Not to be liked, but to be something more than I was.

"Can you take us to the beach?" one girl called to me.

Smiling, I flicked my hand and turned the room into a beach. Soft sand appeared underfoot as the students stood up and went nearer to the calm turquoise water.

Dracian took no notice of the beach, instead watching me closely, his tongue flicking out to lick his lips when our gaze met.

Holding the spell drained my magic, although I brought everyone back to the classroom when Mrs Hinley flapped, her hands literally waving up and down so much, I thought she might take off.

"Well," Dcvon said as everyone settled again. "I think we can safely say that Alishia Jones is a powerful witch, ready to become a good agent with the right training. I wish you all the best."

As I walked back to my seat, I couldn't help the burst of happiness that unfurled within me. If a witch with awesome taste in clothes, and a dagger that could slit Dracian's throat within seconds, saw potential in me, then maybe, just maybe, I could be more than I ever imagined.

10

The bleep of the intercom made me look up. *This is Professor Seaton. After two more student casualties, it has been advised that we suspend all classes until further notice. The ball will go ahead tonight, but it will be heavily chaperoned. Please use this time to study in your dorm rooms and be extra vigilant.*

Shaking my head, I went back to my book. I had decided to come to the library for some peace and quiet. Helissa had been snoring when I left, finally able to rest easier. I hadn't managed to sleep most of the night, so when dawn broke, I had left our room.

Devon Jinx was still in my mind, her words of encouragement making me feel more confident in my abilities. I was determined to master the art of magic in my own way.

"It was you, wasn't it?" a female student said, bringing my attention away from the book.

I looked over the top of Witchcraft for Dummies - What? I needed to start somewhere - and tried not to roll my eyes.

Three witches, two female and one male, stood in front of me, their angry glares giving off a hatred I had never felt directed at me before.

"No," I replied, knowing full well that they were talking about the students whose magic had disappeared.

The girls scowled at me, their arms hung by their side, ready for a fight. What did they want from me? I was in the middle of a library, albeit, a big one with nowhere to run. Did they really think they were going to entice me to fight?

"You need to stop taking other students magic," the male said, cracking his knuckles.

Putting my book on the table beside me, I reached into my pocket and pressed the button on my Electric Beamer. Ugh, needed a proper name for it!

They wouldn't threaten me and get away with it. I was used to blending in with the crowd, but ever since I'd arrived at the academy, everyone had it in for me.

"What do you want?" My words were calm as the electrical current shifted into a magical current within me.

My feet were solid on the ground as I rose. The students stepped back, their stances on alert as I pulled my hand out from under my jacket. A flick of my eyebrows made them clench their jaws.

"You need to be stopped and Seaton isn't doing anything." One of the girls whispered a freezing spell when I lifted my hand.

My whole body went still, the spell settling on my skin like a cloak. Little bitch, how dare she try to incapacitate me when I was trying to reason with them?

"I've not done anything." My words squeezed through my frozen teeth. "Leave me alone."

Fury, hot and heavy, scorched my veins as they laughed. The spell broke as I growled low in my throat. For too long, I had hidden from the world, trying not to be noticed. As soon as I was free, every bugger in the academy had noticed me for the wrong reasons. I was done, I wasn't going to allow anyone to control or threaten me ever again.

Raising my hands, I chanted a spell to send wind spinning around them. The girls grabbed their skirts, trying to keep them from fluttering everywhere. Their hair, which had been so well tended, flew around their faces, blocking their visions. I couldn't hurt them, I would be expelled instantly, but I could shake them up.

"Alishia?" Dracian's voice broke my attention, making me drop my arms.

The wind disappeared as the magic released from my spell. He stepped around the others, his frown pulling his eyebrows low. Without waiting for me to start up again, the male witch took out a knife and threw it. My stomach churned when I ducked, my hands covering my head as I squeaked. I wasn't ready for weapons, what was going on?

Dracian shouted a spell, his voice tight as the witches rushed for me. When I glanced up, I caught sight of the knife, which hovered just in front of my face. The male witch grabbed it, only just lowering it before his momentum sent his body into me. I fell to the floor, unable to defend myself as his fist ploughed into my ribs.

Fire suddenly appeared around us, blocking my view of Dracian. He had been trying to get to me, but the female witches stood their ground. Shoving at the male's chest, I imagined myself as a tiger. When the male witch felt my sides go soft, he looked me in the face, his eyes widening bigger than golf balls. Yes, screw you, preppy academy boy. I was about to eat his face. Well, my illusion tiger was, anyway.

Backpedalling off me, he thrust through the fire barrier that had prevented Dracian from getting to us. When his clothes caught on fire, I extinguished them with a flick of my hand, sending water all over him. I didn't hold back, instead imagining a ton of liquid falling from a cloud above his head.

As he fell to the floor, his knees crippling under the weight of water, the females flew at me, their arms outstretched.

Dracian called a warning, telling me to move. I dove in the opposite direction as the fire barrier dropped. My head just prevented from hitting the floor as I looked up. Dracian concentrated hard on the girls, his mouth moving as he conjured vines. They appeared from under the dark wooden floor, instantly gripping the girls' ankles and tripping them.

"Enough!" Mrs Hinley appeared around the corner of a bookshelf, her expression stern as she marched over. Her short pink skirt matched a bright pink blazer with the academy's emblem sewn on the breast pocket. Tapping it, she shook her head. "Professor Seaton-"

"It wasn't her fault," Dracian interrupted, leaning on his knees to catch his breath.

It would've taken a lot of magic to cast a spell that big, especially for a student.

Apparently, my enemy had just become my frenemy, and he was good at using magic, too. Handy Harry, except for the fact that I didn't want his help. Never. Ever.

The girls squirmed against the vines that bound them.

Mrs Hinley stared at us all, her lips pulled down in a frown. "Alishia," she started. "I did wonder if the academy would be too much for you."

"No," I said, surging to my feet. "I was provoked."

The male witch sat on the floor, sopping wet from head to toe. He glared at me as he spat water when it dribbled out of his mouth. Well, he must have been thirsty after hitting me. I wasn't a punch bag, especially not for a bully boy. He got what he deserved. In fact, he deserved to be castrated. Maybe that was something I could work on. Okay, so that was a little too strong a punishment, but he had almost broken my ribs.

"Get up!" Mrs Hinley ordered the three who had attacked me.

The vines slipped away when Dracian waved his hand to release the spell, allowing the girls to climb to their shaky legs. They held on to each other, both snarling at me.

"You will go to Professor Seaton right this moment. We have not declared Alishia Jones as a suspect, so you mustn't assume that it's her hurting the other students. There's no proof of who it is yet."

The students skulked off, the squelch of the male the only sound coming from them as they walked down the aisle and back to the main part of the library.

Several students watched us from further away, whispering amongst themselves as Mrs Hinley faced me.

Dracian came closer, brushing a hand though his dark waves of hair where they sat on top of his head.

"I'm sorry," she said to me. "But, I simply cannot have you at the ball tonight. Your presence will make it harder for us to try and whittle out the culprit. I'll let you in on a secret," she said quietly, coming closer to us. "We've got Devon Jinx in to help us find the person draining our students."

Putting a hand over her heart, she pursed her lips.

Dracian glanced at me as I clenched my hands into fists.

Not going to the ball wasn't a worry for me. It was actually a blessing in disguise. I hadn't wanted to go to the stupid dance anyway. Isabel might not appreciate Mrs Hinley's ban, but a smile tried to creep across my lips as I nodded, almost violently.

"Fair enough, Mrs Hinley," I said, glancing at Dracian when he snorted. "I promise to stay in my dorm tonight. I could probably get a shift at my job actually."

Slanting her head, Mrs Hinley tutted loudly when her bun almost dislodged. "I'll take care of the students who threatened you. If you have any more trouble, report to Professor Seaton immediately. We won't have any of our students bullied. It might be safer for you to stick to your dorm for study time over the next few days."

Glancing at Dracian, Mrs Hinley narrowed her gaze on him.

He didn't say anything, instead he gave her a big broad smile, one that lit up his face and made his dark eyes sparkle. Oh, the charm that boy had on him was criminal.

Even Mrs Hinley, who was obviously married to the head teacher Seaton, melted under his gaze. Without saying another word, she shook herself and marched away.

"Do you put a love spell on everyone?" I asked him when she was out of earshot.

Picking up my bag, I tried not to cringe as pain blasted my side. Dracian saw the expression on my face and took my arm, holding me as I stood straight again. Slowly pulling away from him, I chucked my jacket over my shoulder. I would have some nasty bruises on my ribs in the morning. Bloody witches, why were they so mean?

"Of course not. Do you need to go to the infirmary?"

His eyes were soft, all kind and caring as if he hadn't killed my parents. Bitterness rose in my throat as I dismissed his kindness with a quick shake of the head. He was getting under my skin and not in the way I thought he would. I had come to the academy to take him down, but instead, I was starting to weirdly like the bastard. That had to change because it just wasn't right.

"I'm fine."

Striding away from him, I paused when he called me back. Looking over my shoulder, I waited for him to speak, my arms shaking slightly from the shock of being attacked. I might play the hard girl, but I had to harden myself, forcing my bottom lip not to tremble. Being bullied wasn't fun.

"Aren't you going to-?"

"Thank you," I said quickly before rushing away from him.

He might not have been asking for gratitude, but I had to begrudgingly give it to him anyway.

Who would've thought? The boy who I'd come to the academy to destroy had made himself my ally. That wasn't something I was comfortable with, so I had to change it somehow.

Leaving the library, I trotted down the steps, keeping my head down. Stares followed me wherever I went. I was truly the infamous Alishia Jones now. My back burnt from their glares as I ran up the steps of the dorm wing and hurried down the corridor. Students hung around, bored from not being able to go to class. Apparently, that was all my fault. How could I prove to these people that it wasn't me?

Unlocking my door, I thrust into our room, dropping my bag on the ground.

Helissa looked up from the book she was reading. A small smile crossed her face as she waved. She had been up and down the last few days, trying to get used to not having a familiar. My suggestion at getting a new snake hadn't gone well. How was I supposed to know that a familiar had to choose its owner? I had never been chosen.

Snapping out of my pity party, I plonked myself on the bed, clasping my side when pain sliced through me.

Helissa noticed, a frown crossing her face as she moved to the edge of her bed. "You look like shit," she said, coming over to sit beside me. "What happened?"

Her demand was harsh, her tone tight. I couldn't ignore her as she rose her eyebrows and gestured for me to answer. Before I could, Isabel waltzed into the room, her high ponytail swinging behind her. As soon as she saw us, her high mood dropped.

"Who beat you up?"

"How did you know?" Trying to sit back on the bed, I cursed loudly.

Helissa jumped up from the bed and went to the chest of drawers that rested under the window. Taking out a small ceramic pot, she came over and offered me a pill.

"I'm not sure that will help, I don't fancy getting shitfaced."

Her snort was followed by Isabel's cough. "Alishia!" Isabel snapped, frowning down at me with an almighty higher than thou expression. "If you would take your head out of your arse for two minutes, you would know that Helissa aced medical magic in high school. I'm sure she's offering you a healing tablet."

Nodding, Helissa urged me to take the small orange pill. "Yes, it's made with natural herbs infused with a healing spell. It will get rid of the pain and bring out any bruising within minutes."

Her face lit up as she spoke, her arms moving in excitement. It was nice to see that Helissa had found her passion. According to Isabel, who was technically right, I had been so engaged with my own affairs, I hadn't even got to know Helissa. Considering they both wanted to help me, and that Helissa's snake was killed because of me, I was being unfair to them.

"I'm sorry," I said as I took the pill and swallowed it down. "I have been preoccupied. I promise to be a better friend from now on."

Glancing at my bedside table, I frowned when I noticed a letter with my name on it.

Helissa followed my gaze, jumping up to retrieve it. "This came for you from Infinity just before you came in."

Taking it from her, I ripped it open. I hadn't let them know that I had contacted the snake-killer, but now was the perfect opportunity. They watched me as I scanned the letter, my fingers tightening on the paper as I read.

"It's from the snake-killer," I whispered.

Helissa gasped in a breath, her hands clenching into fists as she watched me. I handed it to her, not trusting myself to speak. If the mere mention of the boy who had killed her snake made her tense up, I didn't want to be the one to read the letter out to her.

"He wants you to meet him at the ball tonight." Helissa's words were pushed through clenched teeth.

"I sent him a letter, asking him to meet me. I didn't expect him to want to meet at the ball, there'll be too many people there. It's too risky."

Wringing my hands in my lap, I chewed on my bottom lip until blood lined my tongue. The pain in my ribs had disappeared completely. Wow, Helissa was brilliant with healing magic. Maybe I could get her to heal my emotional pain, too. Surely, it wouldn't take too much to drag pain from someone? It was a thought I would shelve for later, even if my therapist had told me that I should always allow my emotions to surface, otherwise it wasn't healthy.

"You've got to meet him. We can be your backup. I've always fancied myself as someone's sidekick." Isabel took my hand, dropping it when heat formed between our fingers.

I wasn't in any fit state to control my ability to take magic from others, so it was best that she didn't touch me. Before Helissa could jump on the bandwagon, I surged from the bed and stood in front of them, hands on my hips. I hadn't bothered to wear my academy skirt, expecting to get changed after I'd finished my early morning revision before class. Now that class was dismissed, I would stay in my jeans and jacket. It was no wonder everyone hated me. No one loved class, but everyone had chosen to come to the academy to learn. Why, oh, why, did my ability, or inability really, have to be my downfall?

"I have to go alone, it says it in the letter. I'm not risking either one of you."

They both went to protest, but I waved my hand, making their voices silent with a small spell. Their faces contorted with anger as they moved their mouths but no words came out. Okay, so it was a little cruel to shut them up, however, no amount of protesting would change my mind.

"I have about five minutes left of magic before that spell runs out," I said. "So, I'll tell you how this is going to happen. Mrs Hinley has banned me from the ball after an altercation between a few witches and myself. Dracian-"

Isabel grabbed my arm, tugging it hard. "Dracian?" she mouthed.

Nodding, I shrugged her off. "Yes, Dracian bloody Dread helped me fend them off. That doesn't matter now." Waving away their silent protests, I went on, determined to say my piece before they could interfere. "So, I'm going to have to sneak into the ball. I can't do that with you guys. If you could help me by being my inside spies, I might be able to lure the snake-killer outside."

My magic ran out, the last withers of it sinking into the floor beneath my feet. Oh great, here came the barrage of abuse from those I was technically protecting.

"He says that he'll be wearing a Phantom of the Opera mask. We can text you to let you know whereabouts he is in the ballroom," Helissa said sensibly.

Isabel nodded an agreement, her ponytail jumping up and down. "Hopefully, you'll be able to bring him down with your magic."

Licking my lips, I debated telling them my whole plan. They were my friends, two people who I was trying to trust, but old habits die hard and all that. When I saw the excited look on their faces, I changed my mind. I had to start to allow people in. If I didn't, well, I would probably end up dead.

"I'm going to lure him outside where I'll cast a vine spell."

"Vine spell?" Isabel interrupted. "That's too hard, how will you do that?"

"We've not even had that lesson." Helissa got up to retrieve her class diary. "It's not until the second term."

Swallowing, I gulped air into my lungs. "I'm going to study it this morning. After I saw…"

My pause made them watch me, their gaze narrowing. I didn't know how to do this, how to open up and not be guarded with what I told them.

Isabel seemed to detect this, her eyes widening as I stuttered. "It's okay," she said, patting the mattress. "You can trust us, we're not going to tell anyone or interfere with your plan."

Taking a deep breath, I exhaled as I sat on the bed. "I saw Dracian Dread use the vines. I want to memorise how to do it, but..."

"But?" Helissa whispered.

"I might have to steal some of Dracian's magic to take down the snake-killer."

11

My heart thudded deep in my chest, reminding me that I was alive as I peeked through the crack in the door. The ballroom was full of first year students, all dancing and eating together. It was strange seeing so many eighteen year olds not grinding up against one another. The one time I had snuck into a club, I had enjoyed the dancing, but any time a boy tried to grind on me, he got a spell or two up his butt. Well, not literally, but my little spells had made them need to retreat to the toilet. I wasn't some prime cow, ready to be plucked and taken home, thank you very much.

Some would say that I was old fashioned, being that I didn't fit into English societal norms, but I didn't care. What was wrong with wanting to respect myself as a woman?

"What are you doing, Magic Fingers?"

His voice made me jerk back from the gap in the doors. Oops, my attention had been so focused on the ball, I hadn't noticed Dracian Dread creep up behind me. That wouldn't do, my agent skills had to be sharp, constantly on alert. Although, they were now fully alert.

Dracian stood in front of me in a navy blue tux and black leather boots tucked under his trousers. The top button of his white shirt was undone, showing just a sliver of tanned skin. My gaze traced upwards, over his strong jaw and to his pretty brown eyes. Why did he have to be so bloody sexy?

"I'm..." How did I get out of this one?

"Why are you not dressed in a gown?" His gaze lowered, examining my jeans and jacket.

It had seemed pointless wearing a pretty dress when I was banned from the ball, even if my stomach had dropped when I saw how stunning the ballroom was. The candles in the chandeliers burnt deep red, sending a glow over the students, who all looked glamorous in their different style of gowns and suits. A part of me wanted to waltz on the dance floor, arm in arm with a handsome man. Alas, I had a job to do... which was why I was actually quite pleased to have run into Dracian.

"You heard Mrs Hinley, she banned me."

My plan to take his magic dropped instantly. How could I use my enemy? How could I use anyone that way? It would be going against everything my father had worked, and probably died, for. He wanted me to have the power of electricity to turn

273

into magic. And, I had that, sitting in my jacket. So, why had I even contemplated the idea of taking Dracian's magic? Did I not trust my own?

"You're an illusionist witch," he said, trying to do up the buttons on his shirt cuffs. "Why not just pretend you're someone else?"

For some bizarre reason, I hadn't even contemplated that. Again, it was because I would be using my magic for bad, not good. My mother had always preached that a gift should never be used for bad intentions, including my own. I had prided myself on not being too reckless with my magic.

"I... can't, I actually have something to do."

About to turn to leave, I hesitated when he extended his arm to me. "Would you help me?"

His cuff was still undone, hanging outside the sleeve of his smart jacket. Automatically reaching for him, I buttoned it, pulling back quickly. Before I could retreat fully, his hand turned, his fingers grasping mine. Heat exploded between our hands, his magic pouring into me. Trying to rip away, I frowned when he wouldn't let go.

"It feels nice," he murmured, releasing me when I growled at him.

His hand stayed in the air as I tucked mine into my pocket. I stared at the ground, ashamed that I had allowed myself to take his magic when I had just vowed not to use him. Why was he watching me as if he could eat me? I wasn't tasty, that much I knew. And, he wasn't a vampire, so the longing was strange. He could have anyone he wanted in the school. Maybe he had cat traits. They always went to the people who hated them, determined to bring them around. Well, I wasn't about to start stroking Dracian. Oh man, bad mental image.

"I need to go." Spinning, I marched across the entrance hall and out onto the steps.

My breath was uneasy as I glanced behind me. Good, the bastard man who had me tingling in all the wrong places hadn't followed me. Hopefully, he would go to the ball and have a grand old time while I got my shit together and somehow lured out the snake-killer. Once he was caught, I could concentrate on clearing my name.

When my phone vibrated in my pocket, I jolted, grabbing it out. Answering it, I kept my voice low as I jogged around the side of the building, towards the rose garden. The ballroom doors opened out into the garden, giving me the perfect place to hopefully take down the boy. As long as we were hidden, which I was hoping I could achieve somehow, all would be hunky dory. Being an agent was harder than I had ever imagined!

"Isabel?"

"I swear, if I trip over this dress one more time, I'm going to rip it off and call myself a naturist."

Coughing, I shook my head as I neared the iron gate that led to the rose garden. "Come back to focus," I said slowly. "I need info."

"Sorry!" she sang, her voice growing lower with her next words. "There's a guy with a phantom mask. He's looking around, inspecting the crowd. I know he told you to wear the same mask, but since you're not here, he's growing impatient."

"I'm going to sneak in from the back for a moment and lead him out."

"But you didn't get dressed up," Isabel hissed down the phone. "Mrs Hinley might catch you."

Unclipping the iron gate, I slipped through. I had planned to go into the ball from the main entrance, using an illusion spell to hide myself, but Dracian had thrown me off guard, forcing me to change my plan. I couldn't risk him sticking beside me once inside the ballroom. Not that he would've done, of course. I was sure that as soon as

277

he'd spotted the gorgeous ladies fawning over him, he would've dropped me like a hot potato.

"Isabel," I interrupted as she started to rant about danger blah blah. "I'll cast an illusion spell, okay? Where is he?"

"I just told you, in the ballroom."

My feet skidded to a halt as I came into the rose garden. Her mind was either elsewhere or she was losing it. I didn't remember her being particularly - what was a kind word? - unfocused.

"Oh, you mean..." She laughed at herself, the sound ringing in my ear. "Sorry, I'm such a numbnut."

Pressing myself to the side of the building, I watched the students through the glass windows. They were slow dancing now, their bodies swaying to the music. It was a good job I wasn't inside, I would have probably fallen over three times already considering I couldn't dance. Well, I liked to think I could, in my bedroom, all alone. But, in company...

"He's standing by the fireplace to the right of the entrance hall, almost directly opposite the windows to the garden." Isabel giggled at something someone said. "Shall I do anything?"

"No," I said, sticking my hand in my pocket. "I've got it from here. Enjoy yourself."

Hanging up, I tucked my phone away and pressed the button on my Witchy Wand, oh I liked that one. The surge of electricity made my body shake, my muscles tightening hard. I was supposed to relax and allow the energy to flow through me, but I was too nervous. As the electricity instantly transformed to a magical current, I cast an illusion over myself.

A gown of baby blue encased my body, a mask of the phantom resting on my face. It was probably completely mismatched, like my fashion sense, but it would have to do.

Wasting no time, I trotted up the small steps that led to the ballroom. Opening one of the doors, I peeked inside.

Mrs Hinley and Professor Seaton were making eyes at one another as they spoke near the altar. My gaze sought the chaperones, who watched the dance floor religiously. My illusion spread to the door, making it look like I wasn't sneaking in as I slipped through it. The teachers wouldn't approve of my tricks, but I had to capture the boy who had killed Toby.

Searching the room, I ducked my head when Dracian glanced in my direction. He was talking to a couple of his friends, including James Hinley-Seaton, who looked around urgently. Tension was in the air, but maybe it was just my own.

When my gaze reached the fireplace, it landed on a boy who wore a phantom mask. He was staring straight at me, his blue eyes bright against the white mask. His suit was the same as the one in the film, although his smaller shoulders didn't match Gerard Butler's. In fact, nothing about him could compare to the hot Scottish actor who was old enough to be my father.

Shaking my head of insane thoughts - who thought about Gerard Butler when in the middle of a covert operation? - I stared back, inclining my head to acknowledge him. He slowly lifted off one foot, starting his journey across the middle of the dance floor.

My hands trembled as I turned and stepped back through the door that led into the rose garden. Keeping my arms to my side, I marched down the steps and across the courtyard, in an attempt to lead him into the roses and out of view from the ballroom. I would need all my magic for trapping the culprit, instead of hiding us from the other students.

"You look pretty in that dress," he called, his voice unfamiliar.

Clenching my hands into fists at my sides, I kept facing forward and released the spell so my normal clothes appeared. His footsteps were loud, closing in on me. As soon as we were hidden from the windows, I spun and faced him. We weren't too far from the fountain, but I didn't want to get too close, just in case he used magic to drown me in it.

"What do you want?" I barked, my voice shaking despite my efforts to calm myself.

Coming to a stop, he crossed his arms over his chest. His clothes fell away from him, revealing ripped jeans and a dirty T-shirt. His hair was scruffy, as if he had been tugging at it relentlessly. Wait, was he a-?

"I want your secret so I can use it for myself." His gaze dropped to the stone under his feet. "And sell it on the black paranormal market."

Wow, it hadn't taken long for another illusionist witch to try and exploit me. My father had warned me of the dangers of going public. Maybe it was stupid of me to join the academy, I should've listened to him. This boy was the same one who had run away from us when we'd found him outside the bar.

Swallowing, I bit my lip before I replied. "I won't allow that to happen. You have no idea-"

"Do you think I care what you want?!" he shouted, his face contorting in rage as his cheeks grew red.

He hadn't made a move towards me yet, but if his trembling was a sign of things to come, he was on the edge. It wouldn't be long until I had to use every part of my magic to bring him down. I just hoped Mother Earth was on my side. One illusionist witch against another was pretty unheard of.

"I've been fighting this, every day, but I can't win!" Rocking from side to side, he clenched and unclenched his hands. "I need more."

Shit, I had heard of magic-addicts but had never come across one. And this particular boy was completely off his rocker. I had to bring him down before he could hurt me.

"I'm sorry," I said, even though I wasn't. "I'll help you, I promise."

Maybe placating him would lead him to trust me. That way, I could trick him enough to try and capture him. I would go to the professor after I'd caught him and ask for his help. He probably wouldn't appreciate that I'd kept it from him but needs must. So far, the so-called head teacher hadn't even bothered to update Helissa on any of their own investigations, which meant he was too wrapped up in the students who were losing their magic. I was doing him a service.

Bulging eyes glared at me as the boy's body started to shake violently. "I'm all out, I need some... please."

His teeth were gritted, his tongue trapped between them. Blood slid down his chin as he stared at me, his breathing rapid and uneasy. He reminded me of a rabid dog my foster parents had tried to rescue. When it looked at me with sadness in its eyes, I had used my magic to put it out of its misery. The poor dog had rubbed his nose against my sleeve just as his soul went back to where it had come from.

I couldn't do that with this boy, he was a fully grown living witch. One who looked like he wanted to murder me and eat me for breakfast. Or dinner, I was probably more of a dinner meat.

"What's going on?"

Dracian's unexpected interruption jolted the boy, sending him flying towards me. I threw up my hands, inciting a freezing spell. He froze in mid-movement, his arms and one leg raised. His jaw was the only thing that was free, allowing him to speak.

"I'll get you!" he spat. "I told you to come alone!"

Dracian came up behind me, his hand resting on my elbow. Pulling away, I glared at him before turning back to the snake-killer.

"Leave us alone, we have business to discuss."

Who was I kidding? I needed Dracian Dread's help. My whole body was shaking as the boy swore at me, spittle flying from his mouth. If I didn't get him now, he would escape.

"No way am I leaving you." Dracian grabbed me back when I went to move towards the boy. "He's crazy!"

Shrugging him off, I yelped when the freeze spell broke, releasing the culprit.

Surging towards me, the boy brought out a gun and aimed it at my head.

Ducking, I screamed as a bullet exploded from the barrel, missing me by inches.

"Stay still, the pair of you!" he ordered.

Both Dracian and I rose to a stand, our hands held up in surrender. The boy aimed his gun at Dracian, his eyes rolling wildly.

I glanced at my apparent saviour, not saying anything when he shook his head curtly. Whatever happened would be my fault. Yes, I wanted revenge on Dracian, but I didn't want to stoop to his level. I would never kill someone to avenge my parents.

"You said you'd help me," the boy said, bringing my attention back to him. "But I know our kind. We're only out for ourselves, never interested in helping others." His arm shook so violently, the gun jerked.

One wrong move and he would shoot. How was I going to get out of this one? I had never imagined that the snake-killer was a crazed boy, desperate for a hit of magic. My detective skills had led us into extreme danger. Maybe this would knock my overinflated ego down a peg or two.

Taking a deep breath, I braced myself. "I want to help you get out of this."

"No!" he hissed through his teeth. "You want to get me into Paranormal Rehab and help me overcome my addiction. I don't want that, give me your secret. Now! Or, I'll shoot your boyfriend."

"He's not my boyfriend," I said, wincing at my automatic reaction.

"Seriously?" Dracian lowered his hands to look at me. "You're so repulsed at the thought of being my girlfriend, you'll risk getting me shot?"

My mouth gaped open, but I had no reply. I couldn't pretend that it wasn't true, the evidence was in my words. However, maybe he was right about me being a little selfish in my reply.

"Sorry?" I offered up, cringing when he shook his head.

"Shut up!" Waving the gun again, the boy almost jumped in the air. "Tell me, bitch!"

Oh no, he didn't just call me a bitch?

"Vines," I said through clenched teeth as I surged forward.

Praying that Dracian had understood what I meant, I went for the boy, ducking when he aimed the gun at me. My run was swift as I threw up an illusion, hiding Dracian behind a wall of fake rose bushes. If the boy concentrated on me, he was less likely to shoot considering he wanted my secret.

"Fuck!" he cried, pulling the trigger.

Shit, I hadn't expected him to actually shoot me, oops. Diving to the left, I managed to dodge the bullet, which thudded into the ground. My heartbeat was so loud in my ears, I couldn't hear what Dracian was calling. Ignoring him, I leapt towards the boy, who was trying hard to follow me with the gun.

"I'm going to kill you!" His words were mixed with tears as they fell down his cheeks.

As I managed to get behind him, I tried my hardest not to feel sorry for his plight. He had threatened my life, tried to kill me. And yet, my chest squeezed hard when he spun and we were face to face, gaze to gaze.

Reaching forward, he planted the barrel of the gun straight into my chest. I took a deep breath before throwing an illusion spell around myself and stepping back. His eyes searched for me, but I was hidden by an invisible cloak of magic. He moaned low in his throat, the sound building as he threw his head back and screamed.

Joining Dracian, I linked hands with him and chanted the spell I had learnt from the book in the library. He nodded, allowing me to use his magic to create thick green vines that surged up from the ground.

"I can use illusion, too!" the boy shouted, shooting in our direction.

We held our ground, dodging out of the way as the vines crept towards the boy.

He turned and started to run, his footsteps pounding towards the grass section of the rose garden. Voices sounded behind us, alerting me to the presence of the professor and Mrs Hinley, who had just rushed from the ballroom, probably hearing the gunshots.

"Keep going," Dracian whispered.

Dropping the illusion spell so the teachers could see us, I chanted harder and louder, willing the vines to catch the boy. As they started to wind around his ankles, bringing him to his knees, he lifted the gun, held it to his head and pulled the trigger.

"No!" I breathed, releasing the vine spell.

Other gasps came from the students as they filtered out of the ballroom.

Tears came to my eyes as I gritted my teeth and tried to steady my breath. How could he kill himself?

Feeling Dracian squeeze my hand, I looked down at it before pulling away gently. My eyes blinked rapidly as I turned from him and ran to the boy, who was sprawled on the ground, blood pouring from a hole in his temple. He had threatened to kill us, even tried to, but he didn't deserve to die like this. No one did.

Touching his hand where it rested on the grass, I sucked back tears. Footsteps sounded around me before a finger tapped my shoulder.

"Please, step away from the boy. We'll need to interview you. Now." The professor looked sad as he glanced at the blood which had turned the green grass brown.

"It wasn't her fault," Dracian said loudly. "He was a magic addict who wanted to know her invention to sell on the black market."

"It's true," Isabel called, producing the notes that I'd received from him. "He was blackmailing her, I have proof."

Helissa stepped forward, in front of the gathering crowd. "He threatened to kill Toby and blow up the school if she didn't meet him alone. Of course, he killed Toby before she had the chance."

Tears dropped from my eyes as my friends came to my rescue. Ever since my parents had gone, no one had ever been on my side. Until now.

"Very well," the professor said, dismissing everyone with a wave. "Get back to your dorms. The ball is over."

Grunts and moans resounded as Mrs Hinley sent me and Dracian with the rest.

We walked close together, not looking at one another. I couldn't be mad at him, he had helped me to stop the snake-killer. Not that I had wanted the boy dead, that hadn't been my plan at all.

"Thank you," I whispered to him as Helissa and Isabel threw their arms around me. He nodded before he disappeared into the crowd.

My friends squeezed me before stepping back and linking their arms in mine, leading me into the throng of people.

"It will be okay," Isabel said, following my gaze as I glanced back at the dead boy. "You managed to solve the first mystery of the academy."

"Maybe," I replied, trying not to let sadness engulf me. "But, at what cost?"

Turning back to the crowd, I stiffened when someone started to scream.

People pulled apart as a female student fell to the ground and started to seizure.

Professor Seaton was beside us in moments, bending to examine the student as she went still.

My whole body shook as I stepped away from Helissa and Isabel. Somehow, I just knew what had happened. Eyes turned to me, wide and judging.

No matter how hard I pretended that the whole academy didn't believe it was me, I had to face facts as Professor Seaton looked up and voiced what we already knew.

"She's been drained of magic."

My whole world collided as my best friends moved to stand by my side.

The other students whispered as accusing stares stabbed into my soul. I was officially an outcast in an academy full of witches who already hated me. And now, they believed I was draining witches of magic.

If I didn't adopt a thick skin and agent skills right away, I might be thrown out of the Undercover Witch Academy for good.

Other Series by Rachel Medhurst

Hunted Witch Agency

Viking Soul

Paranormal M15

The Deadliners Trilogy

Avoidables

Zodiac Twin Flame Series

Author

Rachel Medhurst grew up in Surrey, England. She writes to prove that no matter where you come from, you can be anything you want to be. Your past may shape you, but it doesn't define you. When Rachel isn't writing, she can be found reading and walking in nature.

Printed in Great
Britain
by Amazon